BRIAN PROCTOR

Moonbound Secrets (FTM2)

Contents

Prologue

(DO NOT READ THIS IF YOU HAVE NOT READ BOOK ONE) —Fated by the Moon—

Lyvia Yule looked up from the book she was reading about shifters and their mates. It was something she'd borrowed from the Kraftman house. They have so many books about their race. Her mind had been blown when she'd joined them at their family dinner last night.

When Dustin announced that he and Sharissa were getting married, his brothers bellowed and laughed and told him he was pussy whipped.

Their mother had just said one word… "Why?"

Sharissa had silenced them by telling them her mate was doing it for her. And they'd be wise to take pointers from him, for their mates may also be human, who will have them pussy whipped so fast their heads will spin.

That had gotten a guffaw from the men, but none of them had argued with her. Their eyes had lit up at the prospect of having their own Fated Mate. Even Mrs. Kraftman had seemed excited. She may not like humans, but if they're bonded to the family, she made an exception. And Lyvia could tell the woman adored Sharissa.

The noise she'd heard a minute ago came again. She set the book on the coffee table and walked to the door. She pressed her ear to the door and listened.

"Meew."

Lyvia slowly opened the door and looked down to find a small orange and black striped kitten trying its hardest to climb the stairs of her porch.

"You poor thing," Lyvia whispered. She walked outside and leaned over to pet the kitten. "Where's your mama?"

"Meow."

Lyvia looked up when she heard the mama cat and smiled. "Here's your kitty, pretty mama." The mama looked just like her kitten. "It's chilly out here. Want to bring your babies inside where it's warm?"

The mama cat seemed to be limping, and Lyvia frowned. She scooped up the kitten and then walked over to the mama, who looked up at her kitten in Lyvia's arms.

"Don't worry, I won't hurt him or her." She held the kitten up so she could see and smiled. "Him."

"Meow." The mama cat limped as she rubbed up against Lyvia's leg.

"Show me where your babies are," Lyvia whispered as she watched the mama cat.

Ever since she was a little girl, she has been able to somehow—in a way—communicate with household cats. Her mom said it was the feline in her. And maybe she was right. But either way—the mama cat turned and limped toward a ditch.

Lyvia's heart beat fast in her chest as she followed the mama cat. When they got to the ditch, she looked down and saw a soaked box on its side.

"Only cover you could find, huh, mama?" Lyvia whispered, following the cat down to the box.

Lyvia looked inside, and her heart broke. "Oh, mama. You were moving this one, weren't you? And couldn't hold him anymore. That's why he came to my door. He'd smelled my tiger."

"Meow." The mama cat said as if to say. 'Yeah, you got that right.'

"Okay, well, let's get you and this little guy inside, then tomorrow I'll have my friends help me bury your little ones and give them a proper burial."

"Meow," the mama cat said as she disappeared into the box.

"Oh, mama, I know you want to bring all your babies, but we can't...."

"Meow."

Lyvia sighed and got to her knees to look inside the box. "Oh!" she said excitedly when she saw a kitten move. "There's another."

Lyvia reached in and grabbed the kitten. It was freezing cold, and Lyvia felt her heart skip a beat. She pulled the kitten out of the box and held it against her chest.

"We'll get you nice and toasty very soon," she promised.

The mama cat came out of the box and looked up at her.

"Come on, mama. Let's get you and your babies out of the cold." Lyvia scooped the cat into her arms and carefully made it out of the ditch and to her house without dropping them.

Once inside, she set the mama cat down and looked for an empty box. Lyvia grabbed the box her mother had sent her birthday present, folded in the flaps, then set the kittens inside.

Lyvia found her heating pad and turned it to the lowest setting, then lifted the kittens up and placed the heating pad inside. She grabbed a small towel, put it over the heating pad, and then placed the kittens back inside the box. She then picked up the box, carried it to the couch, and set it between the sofa and coffee table.

"Here you go, mama," she said, lightly tapping the box.

The mama cat walked over to the box, looked inside, then jumped in and started cleaning her kittens.

"Tomorrow, after we bury your kittens, I'm taking you to the vet and having you three looked over. Don't worry, I won't leave you there," she said with a smile.

Lyvia walked over to the door and opened it. She needed to check the box for survivors. With a frown, she went back to the box in the ditch. Lyvia felt each kitten and found them all frozen and not breathing. With a heavy sigh, she walked back to her house.

Out of eight kittens, only two survived the cold. How the mama cat kept them safe for this long was a wonder. Lyvia decided to keep the mama and her babies. But she needs to find a proper name for her; she can't keep calling her mama.

They're so adorable, **Sharissa** gushed as she picked up the kitten who'd almost died and cuddled her.

"Her name is Angel. Because she has a guardian angel." Lyvia smiled.

"So perfect," Sharissa said as she nuzzled the kitten.

"And this little guy I named Tiger, of course." Lyvia grinned.

"What did you name the mama?" Sharissa asked as she petted the mama cat.

"Symone."

"Pretty." Sharissa smiled.

"Well, the hole is dug," Dustin said as he entered the house.

Lyvia looked up at her friend's mate and smiled. He was so tall and sexy; her friend was very lucky.

"Thanks," Lyvia said. "I appreciate it."

Dustin shrugged. "It's sad to see the innocent die, and I was happy to help."

Lyvia and Shar smiled at each other.

Shar gathered the kittens in her arms while Lyvia picked up their mama. The three of them walked to the ditch. Lyvia noticed Dustin had even wrapped the kittens in a cloth and placed them in the hole.

"What should we say?" Shar asked, watching her friend.

Lyvia shrugged. "Rest well, little ones?"

"Good enough for me," Dustin said with a smile as he started covering the hole with dirt.

Sharissa and Dustin helped Lyvia take Symone and her kittens to the vet.

Symone had something in her hip, and the vet was able to remove it but otherwise gave her a clean bill of health. Tiger and Angel were healthy. And since Lyvia saved the babies, they were warm and happy. A few medications for Symone and some clean bandages, and Lyvia was able to take them home.

"I'm glad they're okay," Shar said as she cuddled Angel.

Lyvia smiled at her friend. "I have a feeling you're going to bond with that kitten."

Shar smiled at her. "Can I have her when she's weaned?"

Lyvia tapped her chin as if she had to think about it, then laughed when Shar pouted.

"Of course, you can. Three cats will be a lot for me to take care of. Two will be enough trouble, but at least I'll have company."

"You'll find your mate Lyvia. Just wait," Shar said with a smile.

5

First Sight

Lyvia hates Mondays. Especially when she and her partner and best friend Sharissa Flemmings get called into their boss's office.

"This project is messed up," Mr. Trinkle said, pointing to his computer screen.

"Yes, sir." Sharissa nodded. "We have fixed it several times, but someone keeps unfixing it."

Mr. Trinkle snorted. "How are they unfixing your project?"

"We don't know. It just keeps breaking," Lyvia said.

"Okay, so why don't you fix the problem?"

Lyvia and Sharissa stared at their boss.

"Mr. Trinkle, as we said, we did fix it," Sharissa said, a bit annoyed.

"Someone **unfixed** it," Lyvia said.

"I don't see the problem here, girls. Just fix it again." Mr. Trinkle waved his hand for them to leave his office.

"The nerve of the man," Shar grumbled as they left their boss's office.

"How many times have we fixed it?" Lyvia asked as they headed back to their desks.

"Four times," Shar grumbled.

Lyvia nodded. "Okay. So, let's fix it one more time, and if it's unfixed again, we'll go to corporate."

Shar looked at her, her eyes wide, then burst into laughter. "I really like having you as my partner. My last partner would have advised that we spend our life fixing the problem so we don't get into trouble."

Lyvia chuckled. "I see why she didn't last long here."

Shar nodded.

"Yes, we'll be there this time. Sheesh."

Shar looked up when she heard her mate's voice.

Lyvia smiled at her friend's delighted face.

Dustin smiled when he saw them and went straight to Shar.

"Yes, Raj, we'll be there. Bye," he said with an irritated growl, then hung up.

"Raj complaining about us missing last week's game?" Shar asked as she wrapped her arms around his waist.

Dustin nodded and kissed her. "We better go this time, or he's liable to drag us down there."

She chuckled. "I'd like to see him try."

"Down where?" Lyvia asked, watching them.

"Dustin's friend Raj is a professional hockey player," Shar said with a smile.

"Holy fuck." Lyvia looked up at Dustin. "Can I come?"

"You like hockey?" Shar asked.

Lyvia nodded. "I grew up with it. My dad loves sports, especially hockey. Says it's the only place a shifter can let off steam and not go to jail."

Shar chuckled. "I never thought of it that way. So, I take it you like violence?"

"Only on the ice," Lyvia said with a wide grin.

"Well then, you should come," Dustin grunted. "It will be nice to have someone who knows what's going on so we don't get lost and call the puck a ball."

Lyvia and Shar chuckled.

"Just tell me what time, and I'll be ready," Lyvia said with a wicked grin.

~❋~

This place is crazy! Sharissa shouted over the noise when they entered the stadium for Raj's hockey game.

"I know!" Lyvia yelled back. "Isn't it great?!"

"I know this isn't because she's a shifter!" Sharissa hollered to be heard over the crowd.

Dustin grinned. "Apparently, your friend likes loud and rowdy."

Sharissa nodded, and Lyvia laughed.

"Shar, you don't have to holler; we can all hear you without you shouting."

Sharissa and Lyvia turned in a circle until they found the source of the voice. The Kraftman brothers sat in the second row, waving at them.

"Shut up, Dylan; it's the excitement of the place," Sharissa grumbled.

They could hear all four men chuckle at her response.

"Come on, let's grab our seats." Livia took hold of Sharissa's hand as they walked down the aisle, Dustin close behind them.

"Hey brother, glad to see you made it, finally," Daryl said as he watched Dustin and the girls sit down in their seats in the row in front of the brothers.

"What? You're telling me you came to last week's game?" Dustin asked, looking at his brother.

His four brothers snorted at the same time.

"We were here," Dylan said.

Sharissa chuckled. "Sorry, boys. We… uh… had other things going on last weekend."

"You mean like a wedding to plan?" Dominic asked, batting his eyes at Shar.

Sharissa slapped his knee. "No."

"They were screwing," Dylan said with a laugh and a grunt.

Others around them stopped talking and looked at them. Shar's cheeks turned a bright red.

"Say it louder, Dylan, don't think they heard you in Japan!" Dustin hollered with a growl.

"Sorry." Dylan chuckled.

"So, you chose to screw your mate's brains out over coming here, huh?" Daryl asked with a shake of his head.

Shar turned around entirely and leaned over the back of her chair to be closer to the brothers.

"Dustin and I have decided to start our family, so we were…." She didn't get to finish her sentence.

Dylan and Dominic pulled her from her seat, and the four brothers hugged her with shouts of excitement. Sharissa laughed as each of them kissed her on the cheek.

"Then what the fuck are you doing here?!" Dylan demanded.

Shar chuckled, and Dustin huffed.

"One minute you're criticizing us for not being here, the next you're hollering at us **for** being here. Make up your damn minds." Dustin growled at his brothers.

"Well, that was before we knew you were aiming to give us a niece or nephew," Dominic said with a grin.

"Please make sure it's a nephew. We have no clue what to do with a niece," Daryl said as he helped Shar back into her seat.

Shar smiled at him. "You know we have no control over that. And besides, all you have to do with a niece is buy her pretty things."

All four men laughed.

"Look at us, Sharissa. Do we look like men who buy pretty things?" Drezden asked, motioning to himself and his brothers.

"You never know." Sharissa winked, then turned in her seat.

The buzzer went off, announcing the start of the game.

"This is so exciting," Lyvia said, jumping up and down in her seat.

"Here they come." Dustin pointed to the team coming onto the ice.

"Yay, Raj!" Shar shrieked as she jumped to her feet when she saw his number on the back of a jersey.

Raj Cunningham turned a quick turn and grinned when he saw his friends in the stands. He waved to them, then turned back to the ice. Today is a special game. If they win this game, they're going to the playoffs. His friends' support will make everything that much sweeter when they wipe the ice with this team.

"Pretty fan you have there, Raj." Alec, his teammate, and friend, said, looking up at the stands where Shar stood hooting his name.

Alec was the only other shifter on their team.

Another female voice blended in with Shar's, one he didn't recognize. She must be the friend they'd asked for an extra ticket for. Her voice sent pleasure up his spine, and he shook his head. Can't let a pretty woman or voice distract him.

"She's taken," Raj said, looking at his teammate.

"Both of them?"

Raj shrugged. "Not sure. The blond is, though; she's the mate of one of my best friends."

"Mate?" Alec asked, his eyebrows furrowed.

Raj grinned. "Yeah. You remember the Kraftman brothers?"

Alec snorted. "Yeah, I remember them."

"Dustin found his Fated Mate."

"No such thing," Alec grumbled.

"Oh, but there is. And all the stories are true."

"All of them?" Alec asked with bright eyes.

Raj grinned. "Every last one of them."

The buzzer went off to start the game, and their minds changed from the possibilities of mates to the game.

"Oh my God! Your friend plays rough!" Lyvia said excitedly when Raj slammed a player from the other team against the glass across the ice for the fifth time.

"He does, doesn't he?" Sharissa said excitedly.

"I love it!" Lyvia shouted with enthusiasm.

The buzzer went off, calling for the first intermission.

Shar looked at Dustin. "I've got to pee."

Dustin chuckled. "All right, babe."

"I'll go with you," Lyvia said, getting to her feet. "We can get something to eat and some beer before we come back."

"Get us a beer too," Daryl said, handing Lyvia a fifty.

Lyvia snorted. "I'm keeping the change if I'm late getting back."

Daryl laughed. "Deal."

Dustin handed Shar some money and kissed her before he let go of her hand.

"Oh, my God. Look at that line," Sharissa groaned.

Lyvia groaned, too. "We're never getting out of here."

"We're going to miss the start of the second half," Shar said, bouncing up and down.

"I have an idea." Lyvia took Shar's hand and pushed past the women. "Pregnant lady with a bursting bladder coming through," she said as she pushed people out of her way.

"Hey!" a woman yelled, giving Shar a shove.

Lyvia turned on the woman and growled at her.

The woman saw her silver eyes, and her face paled.

"I said, pregnant woman, coming through. Do you really want me to tell everyone that you shoved a pregnant woman just because you couldn't wait to take a shit?"

The woman's eyes bugged out of her head as she looked at Shar. "I'm sorry," she whispered.

Lyvia grinned. "That's better," she said, then turned and pulled Shar into the next empty stall.

Both women broke into fits of giggles.

Five minutes later, they were in line for refreshments.

"We can't use the same trick here." Sharissa snickered.

Lyvia grunted. "At least I'll be thirty bucks richer."

Shar laughed. "Yes, let's look at the bright side of things."

They finally got to the front and ordered. They loaded the trays and headed back to the stands. They were five minutes late, and the teams were already on the ice.

"Stop screwing around, Raj!" Dustin bellowed as he stood up, waving his fist at his friend.

"Here you go," Shar said with a smile as she handed him their tray.

"Thanks, babe," Dustin said as he sat back in his seat.

Lyvia was so intrigued by what was happening on the ice that she didn't hear the brothers ask for their beer. She saw Raj's number on the back of a jersey and watched in fascination as he slammed the same man against the glass again. Her eyes were glued to him, and she couldn't pull away.

"Lyvia?!" Shar called out, but Lyvia didn't hear her.

Raj and the same man skated toward Lyvia. Her heart pounded in her ears. The man slammed Raj into the glass right in front of Lyvia, and she jumped. When Raj looked at her, time froze. She dropped the tray of beers and didn't hear the Kraftman brothers' screams of rage.

"Uh-oh," Shar said as she watched her friend and Raj. "I remember that look."

Dustin watched the two and chuckled. "They're screwed."

"Mine," Lyvia found herself saying at the same time as Raj.

Lyvia felt her tiger purr as they stared at their mate.

Raj slammed his fist against the glass and called out something she couldn't understand.

"What the fuck?" Dominic mumbled as he watched the two stare at each other.

"Another match." Sharissa smiled.

"In the middle of one of their biggest games?" Daryl asked with a laugh. "He's royally screwed."

Raj continued to stare at the beautiful shifter. His mate. He never thought he'd find her. She looked about as hungry for him as he was for her.

"Come on, Raj, stop flirting with the bunny and get your head back in the game," a teammate called out.

Raj growled. "She's not a puck bunny. She's a friend of a friend, and she happens to be mine."

The man snorted. "Well, I don't care if she's the Queen of Sheba. Get your head back in the game."

His mate walked down the stairs toward him. His eyes never left hers as she placed her hand on the glass, where his hand was still pressed against the other side.

"I'm going to make you mine!" he growled at her.

She smiled at him, and he knew there was going to be a lot of fucking in their future.

"Cunningham!" his coach thundered.

Raj left his mate and returned to the game, but his thoughts were never far from her.

Pheromones

"Here's one that didn't break!" Dylan called out when he found an unharmed bottle of beer.

"Give me that," Daryl said, snatching the beer bottle from his brother.

"Hey, I found it," Dylan huffed.

"And I'm the one out twenty bucks," Daryl growled.

"Fifty!" Dominic shouted with a laugh. "She gets to keep the change because she missed the start of the second half."

Daryl grunted. "She dropped my beer; she should give me my change."

"She found her mate." Sharissa turned to her brothers. "You can't fault her for that."

Daryl snorted. "I guess not. But this beer is mine," he said, popping the cap and taking a long pull from it.

Shar chuckled as she took their three beers and handed them to the other three brothers.

"Hey!" Dustin growled. "No, giving away my beer, woman."

Shar smiled at him. "If you share your beer, I'll let you do that thing you like tonight."

Daryl spat a mouth full of beer all over his legs and started choking.

The others laughed and pointed at Daryl.

Dustin's eyebrow shot up, and he grinned. "Enjoy the beers, brothers," he said, winking at Shar.

"I don't think they're going to make it to the end of the game." Dustin pointed to Lyvia, who was pacing in front of the glass.

"They definitely won't make it home." Sharissa nodded.

Raj slammed someone against the glass in front of Lyvia. She rushed to where he was and pressed herself against the glass.

"People are going to think she's a slut," Dominic said as he watched Lyvia and Raj.

"She's like a tiger in heat," Drezden said.

"She pretty much is," Sharissa said, watching her friend.

"You didn't act like that when you met Dustin," Dominic said, watching Lyvia.

"Shar isn't a shifter," Dustin said, taking hold of his mate's hand. "I sure acted like them, maybe even worse." He grinned.

A loud bang on the glass had everyone in the area jumping in their seats. Raj was trying to break the glass to get to Lyvia. He probably would have jumped onto the glass if he hadn't been wearing ice skates.

"Raj!" Dustin shouted as he jumped to his feet. "Keep your head in the game and your dick in your pants. We'll bring her to you once you've wiped the ice with the other team's heads!"

Raj's head jerked up to Dustin. He snarled and skated away.

"Don't think that will last long," Shar whispered as she watched the tiger shifter skate toward his teammates.

"Look at her." Dylan pointed at Lyvia pacing in front of the glass again, growling.

"She looks like a caged animal," Shar whispered.

"She's not in her right mind, that's for sure," Daryl said, watching Lyvia pace back and forth. Occasionally she would pound on the glass.

"Why couldn't they have met at a barbeque or our place?" Shar asked with a heavy sigh.

"Destiny is a bitch!" Dylan shouted.

"Amen!" Dominic exclaimed as he pounded on his chest.

"I think everyone is freaking out," Shar whispered to her mate.

"It's the pheromones Lyvia is releasing into the air," Dustin said, pulling her against him. "It's what happens when a female shifter finds her mate and goes into heat."

"But you're not acting like a nut," she said, looking over her shoulder at their brothers.

Dustin chuckled. "That's because I have **my** mate," he said, kissing her cheek. "Don't get me wrong, I'm horny as hell and want to fuck you here and now. But I have more control than these yahoos. And I know our friends need me with my head clear."

"Do we have to worry that some other shifter is going to try and mate with her?" Shar asked, watching her friend. "Like with me."

"Ah fuck," Dustin grunted.

"Let's go have her back," Shar said.

Dustin nodded, and they stood.

"Don't touch me!" Lyvia screamed.

Shar looked at her friend. "Get the hell off her, you mongrel," she cried out as she jumped over the bar separating the glass from the seats, and grabbed hold of the man who was pawing her friend. "Find your own mate!" she screeched, throwing the man over the rail and halfway up the stairs.

"That's my mate," Dustin said proudly, pointing at Sharissa.

"Shar," Lyvia whispered. "I can't take this anymore. I need him—like now."

Shar nodded as she held onto her friend. "Soon, Lyvia, soon."

Lyvia screamed a growl, and Raj responded.

"Shit, this glass won't keep them apart much longer," Dustin said as he joined them.

"Then we'll remove Lyvia from his view…." Shar started to say.

Dustin instantly shook his head. "Raj will go insane searching for her."

Shar growled when a man approached them.

"Let me soothe her ache," the shifter pleaded.

"Get the hell out of here!" Shar screamed.

"Look, Human…."

Dustin used his fist to silence the jackass before he said something stupid about his mate. "I'll go talk to Raj. I'll be right back."

Dustin shoved his way to where Raj was seated in the timeout box, waiting to be released back onto the ice. "Raj!" he thundered as he hit the glass behind his friend.

Raj turned to Dustin—his silver eyes wild.

"Keep your head in the game. The sooner you win, the sooner you can claim your mate."

Raj's eyes seemed to clear a little, and he nodded, then looked up at the timer. Once the timer ran down, he jumped back onto the ice and skated as he'd never skated before.

Dustin smiled. Hopefully, he'll keep that in mind and beat the shit out of the other team. Raj would never forgive himself if he let his team down because of his shifter hormones.

Dustin returned to his mate and Lyvia. Two more unconscious men were in the aisle, and his brothers were standing around the two huddled women.

"How's Raj?" Daryl asked, looking at Dustin.

Dustin nodded. "He might make it through the game without killing someone."

Dylan snarled. "If these damn shifters don't leave Lyvia and Shar alone, I'm killing someone."

"What are they doing to Shar? She's already claimed," Dustin asked, watching his mate.

"She's still a Fated Mate," Daryl said. "And with Lyvia letting off all that pheromone, they can smell Shar too—claimed or not."

"Ah, fuck," Dustin growled.

"It's okay, brother," Dominic said, patting Dustin on the back. "She has her brothers to protect her."

Dustin nodded. "Thanks, Bro."

A buzzer went off, and they looked up at the clock.

"Fifteen more minutes of this crazy ass shit," Daryl said.

"Mine," Lyvia growled when Raj skated to the middle of the rink.

"He is," Shar said, holding her friend. "And you can claim him soon."

Lyvia leaned against Shar and purred.

"Okay, that's new." Shar laughed.

"It's her tiger." Dustin smiled. "She recognizes you as a friend."

"And a fellow Fated Mate," Daryl said.

Shar nodded. "Yep, that's what we are."

"Maybe you should start The Fated Mates Club." Dylan laughed.

Shar smiled at him. "Maybe, I will."

"Mother fucker!" Dustin growled when the buzzer went off again.

"What?" Shar asked, looking up at the board with a groan. "Oh, no."

"They're tied, and now they're going into overtime," Dustin said with a growl.

"The Goddesses truly have a horrible sense of humor," Daryl said as he stepped to the side to block another asshole intent on taking one of the women for himself.

"Raj, make the damn goal so you can claim your mate!" Dustin roared.

Raj looked over at his mate and friends. They were protecting his mate from other shifters, ensuring he gets his woman. He smiled and figured he could at least do what Dustin asked.

He turned back to the game and swerved to the left when the man veered to the right. When he saw the opening, instead of taking it, he pushed the puck over to Alec, who spun in a perfect circle with the puck to avoid the assholes coming at him.

Raj could see that the pheromones his mate was setting off were affecting his teammate—but Alec's brain was entirely focused on the game. Unlike Raj, who could barely think of anything but his mate. Shit, he doesn't even know her name.

"Now, Raj!" he heard Dustin holler.

"Alec," Raj whispered.

Alec heard him, and he'd also heard Dustin. He pushed the puck to Raj, and Raj made the winning shot.

Dustin and his party cheered when Raj made the winning shot.

Lyvia was so out of it that she didn't notice her mate had won the game.

"We need to get her to the locker room," Sharissa said as she led Lyvia away from the glass.

The Kraftman brothers formed a barrier around the two women as they walked up the aisle toward the locker room.

"How will we keep the rest of the team out of there?" Daryl asked as they walked down the large hall toward the lockers.

"Call Tate," Shar said, looking at her mate.

Dustin grinned at Sharissa. "My brilliant mate," he said as he pulled his phone from his pocket.

"Should we get Raj?" Dylan asked.

"Believe me, he's already in there waiting for her," Dustin said with a laugh. He turned to his phone when Tate answered. "Hey buddy, remember that favor you owe me for trying to turn my mate against me?"

"Dude, I didn't, and I don't owe you shit. I took care of Vega for you."

Dustin chuckled. "Okay, fair enough. Then I'll owe you a favor. A huge one."

"What's going on?" Tate asked, intrigued.

Dustin told Tate what happened and what they needed from him. The vampire burst into laughter.

"Okay, I'll be there in two minutes," he said, then hung up.

"He's on his way," Dustin said with a smile.

"Lyvia," Shar said, forcing her friend to look at her.

Lyvia looked at her friend and smiled. "You were right, Shar. I do have a Fated Mate."

Shar chuckled. "Yes, and he's waiting for you in there. We'll keep everyone out. But we can't stay here all night. Do you understand?"

Lyvia nodded. "My mate is in there?"

"Yes." Shar smiled.

"Okay," Lyvia said as she entered the locker room.

Shar turned to the others. "Now, we make sure no one interrupts them."

Lyvia took a deep breath as she walked through the locker room. Her heart was pounding out of her chest, and her nostrils were flaring. She could smell him, and her tiger knew he was close.

She walked around the corner at the end of the row and froze when she saw him. He was naked, and his body was perfect. It glistened in the light, and he had so many beautiful muscles. She really does love the physique of a shifter. And apparently, pigs **do** fly.

Raj spun around when he felt her behind him. He'd smelt her the minute she'd entered the locker room.

"You have too many clothes on," he said, then mentally slapped himself.

'Way to go, Romeo.'

She laughed. "Sorry, I was just enjoying your…." She looked him up and down; he knew what she'd been enjoying.

"Come here," he said, spreading his arms open.

She grinned as she ran to him and jumped on him.

Raj laughed as they fell to the floor, her on top of him.

"We need to hurry," she said, kissing his skin. "Shar and Dustin and the other Kraftman brothers are guarding the door. They even called in the vampire."

Raj laughed. It's always good to have friends like them.

"Well, then let's get started…."

"Shut up," she growled.

He didn't say anymore. Before he knew what was happening, Lyvia was naked and sitting on his stomach, her dripping wet pussy leaking on his skin.

"Fuck!" he cried out, then spun her under him and entered her so swiftly the pleasure exploded through his body.

She screamed, and he stopped.

"Damn it," he grumbled.

He should have known she was a virgin. Shifter females don't have sex with just anyone.

Tiger Mates

"Don't stop," Lyvia whimpered, watching the emotions play across his face.

"I should have…."

"You did what we're meant to do. Now fuck me!"

She heard his tiger growl, and their bodies moved as one.

"So good," Raj groaned. Who'd thought he'd ever find his mate?

She's perfect. Beautiful and a tiger like him. Fuck, he wouldn't care if she was a baboon.

He paused in his thoughts. Are there baboon shifters out there?

"Where has your mind gone?" his mate asked.

He looked at her and smiled, then told her what he was thinking.

She laughed. "Not something I would think you'd think about while fucking your mate for the first time. But thank you for thinking me beautiful and not caring if I was a baboon."

He grinned. "I already like you. I think we'll get along great."

She snorted. "I hope so. Because there will be no one else for me."

He kissed her for the first time, and his brain exploded.

"Oh my God," Lyvia moaned against his mouth.

Everything tingled, and the pain had only been there for less than a minute. Now, it was pure pleasure.

His tongue touched hers, and she felt her mind melt. She couldn't think of anything but his kiss, his cock inside her, and the way his skin felt against hers.

"So beautiful," he mumbled against her lips.

She sighed. "You're not so bad yourself."

He chuckled. "I saw the way you were looking at me."

She laughed.

He moved to sit up, and a sensation neither of them had felt before rocked through their bodies.

"Holy fuck," Lyvia moaned.

"Yeah," he said, out of breath.

She moaned when he wrapped her legs around his hips and got to his feet. He slammed her back against the lockers and started fucking her so hard she cried out. Sensations built up and then exploded, taking her to a whole new world of ecstasy.

"Fuck yes," Raj groaned as he slammed into her, hard and fast.

He doesn't even know his mate's name. How can he call it out when he spills his seed inside her?

"What's your name?" he asked as he buried his face in her neck.

"Lyvia," she panted.

"Lyvia," he whispered, chills running down his spine. "I'm Raj."

She smiled. "I know."

He chuckled. "Of course, you do."

Lyvia squealed when he pulled out and set her on her feet. The mischievous look in his eyes had her excited about what he would do next. He spun her around, so she faced the lockers, then pressed down on her back until she was bent over. He entered her, and she cried out his name.

"Holy fucking shit!" he cried out as he fucked her from behind.

"Have you read any books on Fated Mates?" she asked as she grabbed hold of her tits to keep them from slapping her in the face.

"Yeah," Raj said as he leaned over her back. He slid his hand down to her mound and easily found her clit.

"Oooohh," Lyvia moaned as sensations exploded through her body.

"I've been reading them with the Kraftman brothers since we were cubs."

"Right," she moaned. She'd forgotten Raj is friends with the brothers.

"Fuck! I'm going to cum," he said, then suddenly, her front was pressed against the lockers, and his forearms were against hers, their fingers laced together.

"Holy fuck!" she cried out as an orgasm exploded through her body.

When her pussy tightened around his cock, he called out her name, and his seed released deep inside her. She felt the knot form at her entrance, but that wasn't what had her attention. Her wrists were burning, and they felt like someone had set them on fire.

She screamed as the pain seared through her body. He cried out and laid his forehead against her shoulder. She continued to scream as the pain continued to consume her.

"It didn't say anything in the books about this," Raj growled.

Her pain was hurting him more than his own. He hated to hear his mate in so much pain. His tiger growled and whined as the pain continued, and their mate screamed.

Finally, the pain subsided, and a strange feeling flowed through his body. Like he was getting stronger.

"Oh," she whispered. "It's true," she said with a sigh. "Our connection strengthens us."

He kissed her shoulder. "At least we won't have to endure that searing pain again."

She nodded.

"So," he said, nipping at her shoulder. "Dustin said it takes about thirty minutes for the knot to soften. Maybe we can use that time to get to know each other."

She giggled. "Sounds better than standing here in silence."

~ 🐾 ~

Shar cringed when she heard Lyvia's screams.

"What the fuck is he doing to her?" Tate asked, staring at the door to the locker room.

"It's the bonding ritual," Dustin said as he pulled Shar against his chest.

"Sounds like he's killing her," Tate said.

Shar shook her head as a chill ran down her spine. "It feels like someone is burning your flesh." She looked at her own markings.

"But then it feels like you're the most powerful being in creation," Dustin said, kissing Shar's wrists.

"So basically, the Goddesses brand you," Tate said, looking at Shar's wrists.

Shar looked into her mate's eyes. "We kind of thought of it that way too. They do look like brandings."

Dustin nodded. "Maybe it's the Goddesses' way of branding their creations."

"The screaming has stopped," Dylan said as he leaned his head against the wall across from the door.

"Thirty minutes, and they'll be ready to go," Dustin said, looking at his watch.

~🐯~

Lyvia felt the knot soften and sighed. The knot didn't hurt; it was just uncomfortable while standing there pretty much on her tippy toes.

"Want to let our tigers have some fun?" he whispered into her ear.

Lyvia looked at him over her shoulder, and her tiger purred. "Hell, yes."

Raj grinned.

"Have you done this before?" she asked, unsure if she wanted to know the answer.

He shook his head. "Our beasts only mate with their true mate."

"Right." She nodded. She hadn't gotten that far into her reading yet.

"Ready?" he asked, kissing her shoulder.

"Are you going to pull out first?"

He chuckled. "Nope. We're doing this now," he said as he started to shift.

With a wild growl, she let her tiger take over. She fell to all fours, Raj still inside her from behind.

~🐯~

It has been thirty minutes since the screaming stopped," Dustin said, looking at his watch again.

"I hear growls and grunts," Tate said as he pressed his ear to the door.

"Get back, you pervert," Dustin said as he opened the door.

They walked down to the end of the walkway and stopped when they saw two tigers going at it.

"And you called **me** a pervert!" Tate laughed as he turned and left the locker room.

"They're beautiful," Shar said, her cheeks crimson. She could swear she heard the tigers laughing, and Raj didn't even stop…

"Okay, it's time to go." Dustin took hold of Shar's shoulders and turned her from the mating tigers. "You guys have one hour, and we're dragging you out of here whether you're knotted or not!" Dustin called out as they left the locker room.

"That wasn't something I wanted to see tonight," Daryl said as he paced the hall outside the locker room.

"They're lucky." Dylan smiled as he looked at Shar and Dustin. "Even luckier than you two."

"How so?" Shar asked.

"Because they're both shifters and the same species of shifter. They can fuck in their beast forms," Dylan said with a deep sigh.

Shar frowned.

Dustin kissed her cheek. "Don't listen to his stupidity," he whispered in her ear. "You and I are just as lucky."

She nodded but didn't feel as lucky as she had before Dylan pointed out the slight problem to her. She's **not** a shifter.

"Stupid dipshit." Tate slapped Dylan upside his head.

"Damn it, Vampire. What the fuck?" Dylan growled as he placed his hand to the back of his head.

"You just made your sister feel less of a mate because she's not a shifter," Tate growled.

Dylan looked at Shar with wide eyes. "I'm sorry, Seliana. I didn't mean it like that."

Shar shrugged. "It's okay."

"No, it's not," Dustin growled. "I hope when you find your mate, she's a human. Then we'll see where you stand," he said, glaring at his brother.

Dylan's eyes widened and then softened. "I'd be proud to have a human mate," he said, looking at Shar. "If she's anything like you, that is."

Shar chuckled. "Your mate will be her own person. And you will love her, anyway."

Dylan chuckled. "You're right."

~🐾~

"Hey, everyone," Lyvia said with a smile as she and Raj stepped out of the locker room to find their friends waiting for them.

"Oh my God," Shar said as she flung herself at Lyvia.

Lyvia laughed. "I wasn't gone **that** long."

Shar chuckled. "No, I'm happy that you found your mate."

Lyvia smiled up at her mate. "So am I."

Raj grinned and placed his arm over Lyvia's shoulders.

"It was suggested that I start The Fated Mates Club." Shar nudged Lyvia. "You in?"

Lyvia laughed. It actually sounded like a good idea. "Sure, we can get together twice a week and talk about our mates."

"Exactly." Shar laughed.

"I just thought of something," Dylan said, watching the two new Fated Mates.

"What?" Lyvia asked, watching her friend check out her new markings.

"Fated Mates can't be separated for very long, or they can go insane with need," Dylan said.

Everyone stopped and stared at him.

"Which book did you read that in?" Dustin asked.

"Fated Mates and the Bonding," Dylan said.

"Right. I remember reading something like that," Daryl said with a nod. "The bonding must be regular, or the mates can lose themselves."

"Then we've been doing it right." Dustin grinned.

"Eeww, not a vision I needed," Tate gagged.

"Shut up." Shar gave the vampire a shove. In her wildest dreams, she'd never thought she'd be shoving a vampire. "We're trying to start our family."

Tate grinned at her. "You can stop trying."

"Not nice." Shar pouted.

Dustin stopped at his friends' words. "Tate?"

Lyvia's mouth dropped open. "Shar!" she cried out as she pulled away from

Raj and attacked her friend.

"What?" Shar asked. "I don't understand why you're all looking at me like that."

"Shar, Mafilia," Dustin said as he pulled his mate from Lyvia's arms.

He could hardly believe what his friend was saying. But if Tate has sensed something. He looked up at his friend. The vampire nodded, and Dustin burst into tears. What the hell? He doesn't cry!

"What's going on?" Shar asked, staring at Dustin.

"Shar, you're already carrying my cub," Dustin said as he kissed her.

"I hope you're not playing a joke here, Vampire," Daryl said with a growl.

Tate grinned. "She's just over a week pregnant."

"That's when I stopped taking my pill," Shar squealed.

Dustin chuckled. Their first time making love with her off the pill had created a life.

"Twelve more weeks," Lyvia said with excitement.

"Do you think we started ours, too?" Raj asked, pulling Lyvia against him.

"Oh God," she said, looking up at her mate. "I hadn't even thought of that."

"Tate?" Raj asked, looking at the vampire.

"What am I, the cub guru?" Tate grumbled as he walked over to Lyvia and sniffed her neck. "Nope, not yet, Raj."

Lyvia sighed with relief.

Raj looked at his mate. "Do you not want to have my cub?"

Lyvia looked at Raj and shook her head. "Oh no, I do. But I hoped to get to know you first."

He smiled at her. "How about we start with me taking you to dinner tomorrow night?"

She nodded. "Yes, I would like that."

"Wait a minute. What did you mean by twelve more weeks?" Shar asked. "Don't you mean nine more months?"

Everyone looked at her.

"Sharissa, Mafilia," Dustin said, holding her close. "Shifters are only pregnant for thirteen weeks."

Shar's eyes bugged out. "But I'm human."

"Doesn't matter." Tate smiled. "You're carrying a cub, not a baby," he reminded her.

"Twelve more weeks, and you'll be a mama."

Captain Crunch Berries

"I can't believe no one noticed I wasn't at the party," **Raj said as** he, his friends, and their mates sat around in Dustan and Sharissa's house.

"That's the great thing about having a vampire for a friend," Dustin said with a smile.

"You **both** owe me for this," Tate said, taking a sip of his scotch on the rocks.

"We didn't finish discussing what those two will do when Raj has to go to his next away game," Dylan said, pointing between Raj and Lyvia.

"I can talk to Mr. Trinkle and come up with an assignment she can do from home," Shar said.

"I can't let you do that." Lyvia frowned.

"Trinkle may be an asshat, but I've worked under him for years. I know what he likes, and I can play at his ego." Shar smiled.

"That's actually a good idea. If Lyvia can work from home and email you her work, then she can travel with Raj and the team," Dylan said with a nod.

"And how will we get her on the bus?" Dominic asked his brother.

Everyone looked at Tate.

"What the fuck?" Tate said, watching his friends. "Have I become the local hypnotist?"

"We could use your help again, Tate," Dustin said. "Unless you want them to go insane and probably kill us all in our sleep."

Tate snorted. "Not likely. But I'll help, anyway."

"Thank you," Lyvia said happily.

"You'll owe me too for this one." Tate pointed at Lyvia.

Lyvia nodded. "Anything."

Raj pulled Lyvia away from Tate. "Never tell a vampire "anything" when you owe him a favor."

"Too late." Tate grinned. "She said it, can't take it back."

"She didn't know," Raj growled.

"Relax, Shifter," Tate said with a shake of his head. "I won't have her cut off her own head or anything like that…."

"Didn't you have that one guy do that?" Dustin asked, watching the vampire.

Tate laughed. "That guy raped and beat a young girl almost to death. And since he owed me an 'anything' favor, I told him to chop off his own head."

Both women in the room sucked in shocked breaths.

"He had it coming," Tate said with a flick of his wrist.

"I don't think they're shocked you had a man like that kill himself." Dustin laughed. "I think they're shocked that the man actually did it."

Both women nodded.

"Well," Tate said with that wicked grin of his. "I can be **very** persuasive."

"I believe that," Lyvia said, having been under his control once before when she'd first met him.

"Hey, this is supposed to be a celebration!" Raj shouted. "I found my mate," he said, kissing Lyvia. When he lifted his head, he grinned down at her. "And we're going to the finals!"

The room erupted in cheers, and they went back to celebrating.

Lyvia looked at her email, and her eyes opened wide. Sharissa had done it. She'd actually pulled it off. She looked at Symone, who was rubbing against her leg.

"What am I going to do with you?" she whispered.

Symone looked up at her with a blank stare.

"Thanks, you're a lot of help." Lyvia laughed as she leaned down and petted her new cat. "I guess you're hungry." She got to her feet and went to the kitchen to get the food she'd bought for Symone.

"Good morning, Mafilia."

Lyvia looked up from pouring food to smile at her mate. "Morning, Mafilio."

"Please tell me that's not our breakfast," Raj said with a teasing smile as he pointed to the food Lyvia was pouring for the cat.

Lyvia chuckled and shook her head. "No. Our breakfast is in the cupboards."

"Let me guess, bran flakes," he said with a teasing glint in his eyes.

She smirked at him. "You'll have to see for yourself."

He went to the cupboards and chuckled. "Captain Crunch Berries, nice," he said as he pulled the box down.

He found two bowls and two spoons.

Lyvia chuckled. "Did you forget that I need **my** sugar, too?"

He snorted. "I've met shifters who don't have sugar in their house. But of course, they're also not as toned as you," he said the last part as he turned and winked at her.

She crossed her arms over her chest and glared at him. "I don't want to know about your other morning afters."

"Don't have any," he said as he set the bowls and box of cereal on the dining room table.

"So, you're one of those who sneak out before sunup, huh?" Lyvia asked as she grabbed the milk from the fridge.

When she backed up, she found something very hard at her backside.

"I don't want to talk about my life before you. Do you?" he asked, rubbing her hips through her nightshirt.

She swallowed. "No, not really."

He pulled her to a standing position and turned her toward the table. She set the milk beside the bowls and squealed when her shirt went up, and her panties went down.

"I love your ass." He grinned as he smacked it.

Lyvia groaned. She never knew a slap on the ass could be such a turn-on.

Raj fell to his knees and opened her sweet pussy so he could see it. It was the most amazing pussy he had ever seen. An amazing pussy on an amazing pussy cat.

He heard Lyvia purr and grinned, then leaned up and licked her sweetness, which was already dripping down her thighs.

"Holy fuck," she breathed out when his tongue touched her.

He chuckled. "You like to say that. Don't you?"

She sighed with pleasure. "It's something that has always just popped out of my mouth. Oh God, don't stop."

He chuckled against her clit, his tongue swirling around it. "You taste and smell like apricots."

"What is it with fruit?" Lyvia asked, then cried out when he pulled her clit into his mouth and sucked on it.

Her orgasm came fast, as Raj knew it would. She shook and cried out with pleasure as she called out his name. His cock jumped to attention, and his tiger growled, wanting to mount his mate again.

"Not this time," Raj mumbled to his tiger as he stood and pulled his boxers down to free his cock. She was already bent over the table, still writhing from her orgasm. He slapped her ass cheek, which made her squeal. He grinned as he grabbed her hips and entered her.

"Holy fuck!" she cried out, making him chuckle.

He really likes this woman; he's glad she's his mate. His tiger is happy, too, if the constant purring in his head said anything.

"Damn, you feel good," he said with a groan as he slammed into her tightness.

He was her first, which was a bigger turn-on than any aphrodisiac. To be your mate's first lover is a powerful feeling. He just wished he'd realized it before he'd plowed into her their first time.

"Raj, oh God, Raj, yes." Lyvia let out a loud purr.

He smiled. Her tiger was as happy as his.

"Lyvia," he moaned as he held onto her hips and fucked her over her dining table.

"I can't believe we're fucking in my kitchen," she panted.

He chuckled. "We're going to fuck everywhere in this house before we have to leave for my next game."

She snickered. "That sounds like a good plan to me."

"What did you mean about the fruit comment?" he asked when he remembered her earlier statement. He'd been so involved with eating her that he'd forgotten to ask about it.

She snickered as she turned her head to look back at him. "Sharissa smells like peaches to Dustin."

He smiled. "I guess it's a Fated Mate thing."

She nodded as she turned her head forward again.

"No, I want you to look at me like that." He grabbed hold of her hair and turned her head to face him.

Her eyes became a smoky grey, and he groaned.

"You're so beautiful." He leaned forward and kissed her.

She moaned against his lips. "So are you."

He chuckled against her mouth. He wasn't usually keen on being called beautiful, but from his mate, it sounded perfect. Even his tiger liked it.

"Harder," she groaned.

His tiger pounced, and Raj had to use every strength he had to keep him from taking over and screwing their mate against the table while she was still in human form.

"Not going to happen, buddy." Raj chuckled.

"What's wrong?" she asked, watching him.

He grinned at her. "My tiger got a bit excited when you said that."

She smiled. "My tiger is clawing to come out."

Raj leaned forward so he could whisper in her ear. "Next time, my little tigress, next time."

Lyvia's body exploded with sensations when he whispered into her ear. Her tiger was purring so loud she could barely hear anything else.

"Yes!" she cried out when his arms came down on top of hers, his fingers laced with hers as he pinned them to the table and fucked her harder, just as she'd asked him to. "More." She grumbled, and he slammed even harder and deeper.

"Holy fuck!" she screamed as the biggest orgasm she had ever had erupted from her spine.

"Yes!" Raj called out when she tightened around him. He grunted and slammed into her a few more times, then his body shook with his orgasm, and he spilled his seed deep inside her.

Their joined wrists tingled as their strength joined and multiplied.

"That was…." He started to say once he collapsed against her.

"Incredible," she finished for him.

He chuckled. "That's one word to use."

"Hungry?" she asked, looking at the milk and cereal.

"Yeah, even more now," he said, kissing the side of her neck.

Raj sighed as he watched Lyvia fix their cereal bowls while he was still knotted inside her. He knows she's not ready to start a family with him, and he understands. But the Goddesses intended for them to have large families—hence the knotting.

He'd tried slipping a condom on once, which had never been a problem before. But it had bounced off his dick and slapped her in the face. Which he hadn't been able to hold back his laughter—because come on—Who could have?

She'd punched him, then tackled him to the bed and fucked him from on top. That knotting had been fun. She'd fallen asleep on top of him while they waited, and he slept with his mate's breasts pressed against his hard chest.

"Shar found a job I can do at home," she said around a mouthful of cereal.

He chuckled. He loved that Lyvia wasn't petite 0r against sugar and exercise.

"That's good," he said, shoveling a large bite of cereal into his mouth.

It should be strange to stand behind his mate with his cock stuck in her pussy—eating Captain Crunch Berries. But he found it about as normal as normal got for a shifter with his Fated Mate.

"It's work that will take up a lot of my time, but I should be able to give you my attention on breaks…."

"Screw breaks," Raj said through a mouth full of cereal. "I'm going to fuck you while you're working, and we'll lay or stand together while we wait for the knotting to finish, and you can continue your work. Then we will do it again."

She giggled.

"I guess it's twice as hard for us then it is for Shar and Dustin—since she's human and can only take so much. I mean, the pull is stronger for me because I'm a shifter and all." Lyvia said as she spooned another bite of cereal into her mouth.

Raj laughed at that. "Don't underestimate a human Fated Mate, Mafilia. You forget she has the strength of a shifter now."

"Right," Lyvia said with a nod. "I love Shar with all my heart, and I know how strong she is for a human. But does she have the sexual appetite of a female shifter?"

Raj set his bowl on the table and leaned forward. "From what Dustin's brothers have told me, they've caught those two in bathrooms, the gym, their mother's house, the pool, the jacuzzi...."

Lyvia laughed. "Okay, okay. So, she's got it all and then some. But can she do this?" she asked with a wicked grin. She'd felt his knot softening and knew she better do it now, or her tiger will give her hell all day. She shifted and could hear Raj growling behind her.

He shifted, and her table didn't survive.

Trouble at the Dive

I can't believe you found your mate," Sebastian Bensing said, glaring at Raj. **"You** out of the rest of us."

Raj grinned. "Fate is a bitch."

"You can say that again," Daryl grumbled from the other side of the table.

"But she's a smart bitch. I mean, look what she gave us," Dustin said, watching Sharissa and Lyvia.

Raj nodded with a wicked grin as he watched his mate lean against the bar while she waited for their drinks.

"At least Marry-Beth likes our little human," Daryl said with a smile.

"I think she's jealous." Dominic chuckled. "She keeps looking at the girls, then over at you two with that evil eye of hers."

"She's a lot older than us and hasn't found **her** mate." Daryl waved to the owner of The Shifter Dive.

"Do they have Fated Mates for lesbians?" Drezden wondered out loud.

The others at the table looked at him and broke into laughter.

"You know I've never thought of that." Dustin shook his head.

"What are you boys hackling about?" Sharissa asked as she set a tray of drinks on the table.

"Just wondering if the Goddesses created Fated Mates for the same-sex as they did us." Dustin smiled as he pulled Shar onto his lap and kissed her.

"Same-sex?" Lyvia asked as she sat in the chair beside Raj.

"Yeah, you know," Dylan said, making both fists into O's and pounding them together.

"Oh God," Shar said, staring at Dylan.

He just smiled at her and kept pounding his fists together.

"We get it," Lyvia growled.

Dylan chuckled and lowered his hands.

"I didn't know Marry-Beth was a lesbian." Shar turned her head to look at the bar's owner.

"No wonder she's been looking at **us** with longing instead of the guys," Lyvia chuckled.

"Well, it's time for me to go," Sebastian said, looking at his watch.

"But you just got here," Raj said, watching his friend.

Sebastian shrugged. "We're leaving early in the morning. I just wanted to meet your beautiful mate and tell her she's with the wrong guy," he said, winking at Lyvia.

Lyvia smiled at him. "In your dreams, panther."

Sebastian's hands went to his chest. "Right through the heart, darlin'."

She chuckled. "I was actually aiming lower."

"Ugh!" Sebastian grunted as he backed away from the table. "And at that note, goodnight, all. I will be back next month. You all better keep your eyes in the back of your heads because no one else is finding their mate until I get mine."

"You're dreaming if you think I'm going to not look for mine while you're gone," Daryl growled.

Sebastian snorted, then looked at Raj and Lyvia. "Congrats, you two. And to you two on the cub," he said, smiling at Dustin and Shar.

"Be safe," Shar said from Dustin's lap.

Dustin laid his hand over Shar's flat stomach and grinned at Sebastian.

"And you," Sebastian said, pointing at Raj. "You've got yourself a good mate there. Don't screw it up."

Raj grinned and pulled Lyvia against his side. "Don't plan to."

"Catch you all next month," Sebastian said, then he was gone.

"I've got to pee," Shar said with a moan. "I think this cub uses my bladder as a trampoline."

Dustin chuckled as he kissed her cheek. "Will you go with her?" he asked, turning to Lyvia.

"Of course," Lyvia said as she got to her feet.

Shar jumped off Dustin's lap, and the two women headed to the bathroom—arm in arm.

"They keep looking at our mates like they're a course in a seven-course meal," Raj growled when he noticed almost every eye in the bar on their mates.

Dustin nodded. "You've got to get used to it, brother. It's the pheromone they put off. Mostly your mate. I think she's in heat."

Raj snorted. "Yeah, I think her tiger is. But Lyvia wants us to get to know each other before we start a family. But with the knotting, I don't think that will happen."

"I know Shar will love to raise our cub with her friends. Hell, maybe they'll be mates," Dustin said with a laugh.

"Have you tried condoms?" Dylan asked.

Raj snorted and tried not to laugh. "Yes, and I can't wear condoms with my mate."

"Odd," Daryl said without looking at Raj.

"What happened?" Dustin asked, watching Raj. "I haven't had the need to try with Shar."

Raj snorted. "The condom popped off the tip of my dick and hit Lyvia in the face."

The table erupted in laughter.

"Yeah, I laughed too. Until she punched me. But the sex was awesome after that." Raj grinned.

"How's her tiger taking to all this?" Dominic asked.

Raj laughed when he thought of her dining table. "Let's just say she's as eager as her human to fuck like rabbits."

The men around him laughed again.

"I don't think so," Dustin said, jumping to his feet.

Raj turned to where Dustin was looking and growled deep in his throat.

Five shifters were waiting outside the women's bathroom.

"What the fuck?!" Raj bellowed as he jumped to his feet.

"Let's go stop them before the girls come out," Dylan said as he got to his feet.

"I swear to the Goddesses, I'm not bringing my mate here anymore," Dustin said, cracking his knuckles.

"And what has you fine men in a huff?" Marry-Beth asked as she walked up to the six shifters who looked ready for a brawl.

"Oh, nothing much, just some pricks trying to hone in on our mates," Raj said, pointing to the five men waiting outside the women's bathroom.

Marry-Beth looked at the five shifters outside the bathroom and rolled her eyes. "They could be waiting for **their** women."

"Seriously, you're going to take their side?" Dustin asked, glaring at the owner.

"I'm just saying," Marry-Beth snapped.

"Look, Marry, I know you're jealous that we've found our mates," Dustin said, making the woman glare at him. "And I pray that someday you find yours," he said, raising his hands in the air. "But Shar's pregnant, and I'm not going to let those assholes touch her."

Marry-Beth sighed and let out a growl. "Take it outside. I don't want a single table or chair broken." She turned to leave, then turned back with a genuine smile. "Congrats on the cub, Dustin," she said, then turned and walked back to the bar.

"You heard her boys. We take it outside," Daryl said, cracking his knuckles.

~ 🐾 ~

There's a bunch of guys outside the door," Sharissa whispered as she turned to look at Lyvia.

Lyvia moved from the dryer to her friend and peeked out the door. "Holy fuck."

Shar giggled, and Lyvia rolled her eyes.

"What do you think they want?" Lyvia asked.

"Us," Shar whispered.

"Seriously? Knowing we have two powerful—mate bond pumped—

shifters?"

Shar laughed. "I like that description of our men."

"Let's stay in here until they're gone. I don't want to fight off handsy men." Lyvia walked over to the chairs against the wall and sat down.

"Yeah, I have my cub to think of now," Shar said as she joined Lyvia.

Lyvia laughed.

"What?" Shar asked, looking at her friend.

Lyvia shook her head. "Nothing. I just remembered how I'd used the excuse of you being pregnant, and we didn't know that you really were."

Shar chuckled. "How long should we wait?"

"If they're not gone in five, we'll call the guys."

~🐾~

"Ask them what they're standing there waiting on," Dustin whispered in Dylan's ear.

Dylan nodded and walked up to one of the five men outside the bathroom.

"Good call," Raj whispered.

Dustin nodded, and they watched as Dylan approached the men.

"Hey, man," Dylan said as he stopped beside the shifters. "What are you guys waiting out here for?"

The man closest to Dylan looked at him and laughed. "Haven't you heard about them? There are two unclaimed Fated Mates in the bathroom. I've heard that even if you're not their Fated Mate, the sex is incredible."

"Mother Fucker!" Dustin hollered so loud that everyone in the bar turned to him and his group.

"Oooo, wrong answer," Dylan said as he returned to his brother's side. "Because you see, my brother here is, in fact, mated to one of those women. And our friend here is mated to the other. Soooo... You're screwed."

"Nice speech," Dominic said with a roll of his eyes.

The five men outside the women's bathroom growled.

"Outside!" Marry-Beth shouted at them.

"Why, so they can claim the mates? Don't think so," one of the five men said. "I'm going to fuck that blond human until she bleeds," he said, grabbing his crotch.

"Sorry, Marry-Beth!" Dustin hollered with a feral growl. "I'll pay for the damn tables and chairs!" Before the man knew what was happening, Dustin had him in the air and across the bar toward the exit.

"Holy shit," Dylan said as he watched the bear shifter fly across the bar. "I really need a Fated Mate of my own."

The man landed on an empty table, thank God.

"You better pay for that, Dusty!" Marry-Beth shrieked.

"Here." Daryl slapped a wad of cash on the bar. "For that table and anything else, he may break on his way out the door with that asshole."

Marry-Beth sighed. "I heard what the jackass said about Sharissa. Make sure he pays," she said as she pulled the money to her.

Daryl nodded. "Don't worry. He's going to wish he'd never laid eyes on my little sister."

Marry-Beth nodded. "Just please take it outside."

"Yes, ma'am." Daryl returned to his brothers to help them escort the other four men outside.

"Dustin," Raj said as he took hold of his friend's arm.

"Let me go, Raj," Dustin growled.

"Don't kill him, Dusty," Raj said, tightening his grip.

"You heard what he said about Sharissa. What if he'd said that about Lyvia?" Dustin growled, glaring at his friend.

Raj nodded. "Yes, I heard. And we will kick all of their asses. But you need to remember. If you kill him, you'll go to jail. And what will Sharissa do alone with your cub while the both of you go insane from not being near each other?"

Dustin grumbled. He hated it when people were right, especially when his cougar wanted out of his cage.

"Oh, is a fight a-brewing?" Everyone turned as Tate dropped down from the roof. "I do love a good fight. What are we fighting about today? Taxes?"

"What the fuck, Tate?" Dustin asked, staring at his friend.

Tate smiled. "I was just checking on my favorite mates. Oh, look, that bear looks like he wants to tear off your head, Dusty. What did you do?"

"He threw him across the bar." Dylan chuckled.

"Hmm." Tate looked Dustin up and down.

Naturally, cougars aren't as strong as bears, especially in human form. But Dustin must be getting plenty of lovins from Sharissa.

"And why would he do that?" Tate asked.

"Because he said something about Sharissa," Dylan said.

Tate moved closer to Dustin. Part of his job in this world is to keep shifters from killing each other for stupid reasons.

"What did he say, my friend?" Tate whispered.

Dustin told Tate what the asshole had said and what the five men had been doing outside the women's bathroom. Dustin knows what Tate's so-called job is when it comes to shifters. But right now, he didn't care if Tate tore off his arms. He can bite the stupid ass's head off **without** his arms.

Tate clucked his tongue and looked at the bear shifter. "Looks like you have bitten off more than you can chew, Bear."

"Fuck off, Vampire!"

"Don't kill him, Dustin. I don't want to spend the night trying to explain to the elders why you can't spend time in prison," Tate said as he backed away.

With an angry growl, Dustin took off after the bear. The two men fought as if their lives depended on it, and maybe Dustin's life did. Because the bear had no worries about spending time in prison. But Dustin can't be away from Sharissa for too long before they both go mad.

With his extra strength from his mate, Dustin was winning—until the other four jumped in.

Fierce Tigress

"They're gone," Lyvia said as she opened the door.

"What was that loud crash?" Shar wondered out loud as they left the bathroom.

"Not sure, but I could swear I'd heard your mate hollering."

Shar nodded. "I did too."

They stopped when they saw the chaos of the bar. Tables and chairs were splintered all over by the entrance, and people were gathered by the door.

"Where are our guys?" Lyvia asked, staring at their empty table.

"I have a feeling that's what everyone is trying to watch," Shar said, pointing to the group at the door.

Lyvia looked at the group and nodded. "Let's go see what our mates got themselves into."

Sharissa nodded, and they headed for the front door.

They had to push through the crowd. Two men grabbed them before they got to the door.

"Holy fuck," Lyvia said when she was pulled against a solid chest.

"Get your hands off me!" Sharissa yelled.

"Let them go, you idiots!"

Lyvia and Shar watched as Marry-Beth hit the one holding Shar over the head with a baseball bat.

"What the fuck, Marry-Beth?!" the man cried out as he let go of Shar.

Lyvia kicked her captor in the shin, and when he let her go, she collapsed against Shar.

"Can't you jackasses see they're claimed?!" Marry-Beth shrieked as she pointed to the two women's wrists.

Both men looked at the women's wrists, and their skin paled.

"Looks like I need to put up a new sign," Marry-Beth said, watching Shar and Lyvia. "I don't want those boys to stop coming in here, and if their mates are attacked every time they come here, they're going to stop coming here. And I know Sebastian will follow." She shook her head.

"New Bar rule!" Marry-Beth shouted over the noise of her bar. "Check wrists before you listen to your cock and try to claim them for yourself! The next person to attack a claimed mate is getting their dick mounted on the wall for all to see!" she turned to walk away, then turned back.

"And no cockblocking. If you try to steal someone's mate, more than your dick will be mounted on the wall. If she's not your mate, stay the fuck away from her!" Marry-Beth shouted.

"Or him," Sharissa said when she saw Mable.

Marry-Beth followed Sharissa's eyes and growled. "Or him." She rolled her eyes in agitation and returned to the bar.

"Let's go," Lyvia said as she took hold of Sharissa's hand.

They excused themselves through the rest of the shifters trying to see what was going down outside. Lyvia and Shar made it outside just as four shifters jumped Dustin as he was beating the crap out of another.

"Dustin!" Sharissa screamed as she took off toward her mate.

"Whoa there, little mama," Tate said as he gently wrapped his arms around Shar.

Dustin heard his mate scream, and his cougar took over—no if ands or buts. With a loud, angry growl, he shifted and flung the other shifters off him.

"Shit," Daryl said as he watched his brother. "If he gets caught, he'll be arrested."

"Why?" Shar asked, tears running down her cheeks.

"Because even though humans tolerate our presence, they have one rule," Dylan said.

"Don't shift in public," all six shifters said simultaneously.

Shar looked at her brothers. "Help him," she ordered.

The brothers laughed. "Yes, ma'am." They said at the same time, then went after the shifters who were still trying to take Dustin down.

"Don't kill them!" Tate hollered out to the Kraftman brothers and Raj.

"What started this?" Shar asked as she watched her mate fight a shifter who'd shifted into a bear.

"The bear your mate is fighting threatened to fuck you until you bled," Tate whispered into her ear.

Lyvia sucked in a shocked breath, then picked up a rock and threw it at the bear.

The rock hit the bear in the head and bounced off. The bear stopped its attack on the cougar and turned to them.

"Holy fuck," Lyvia mumbled.

"Good going," Shar grumbled. "You just pissed off a bear."

The bear headed toward them, and Lyvia shifted. When the bear got to them, the tigress was ready for him.

"Damn it, Lyvia!" Raj yelled as he watched the bear rush at his mate.

"Tate told us what the asshole said about me!" Sharissa yelled.

"Great, blame me," Tate grumbled.

"Damn it, Vampire," Raj said as he ran toward them. "Did you forget about the Mate Bond?"

"Not at all." Tate grinned. "I knew she was dying to get involved."

Raj growled at the vampire, then paused to watch his mate as she jumped on top of the bear and brought him down. Her teeth sank into the bear, and the bear roared.

"Get off my man!" a woman hollered as she ran out of the bar.

"Your man?" Raj asked, staring at the woman.

"He'd left the table to go to the bathroom, and when he didn't come back, I went looking for him and heard he was attacked by a pack of hyenas."

"Hyenas!" Shar screamed. "Cougars!"

The woman looked at the cougar helping his brothers take down the other four men.

"Why are they fighting?" the woman asked. "And why is she still on top of my boyfriend?"

"Miss, I think you should sit down." Tate chuckled.

"Fuck you, Vampire. Shouldn't you be stopping this?"

"I told them no killing; that's good enough," Tate said.

"Why are you holding that human?" the woman asked.

"Curiosity killed the bear," Tate said with a wicked grin.

"Were they fighting over a damn human?!"

"Watch it," Raj said, walking toward her. "That human happens to be my friend's Fated Mate."

Her eyes ran from Raj to Shar and back again. "So, they **are** fighting over her?"

"Not fighting over her." Tate's grip tightened around Shar when she moved to help Lyvia.

The bear shook the tiger off. Lyvia landed on her back, rolled over, and stood with a growl.

Raj told the woman what her "boyfriend" had said about Shar, and the woman growled loudly.

"Are you sure she's mated to the cougar?"

Tate held Shar's arms up so the woman could see the markings.

"If you guys had been here a couple weeks ago, you'd have heard Dustin's announcement." Raj walked toward his mate and stood between her and the bear.

"Let me handle this," the woman said, then shifted into her bear and attacked her boyfriend.

Which they were pretty sure was going to be dumped like a sack of rocks.

Sirens rang in the night, and Raj looked at Lyvia. "Shift back," he said.

Lyvia shifted back to her human form.

Raj grabbed Lyvia and pulled her against him.

"That was very stupid," he said, holding her.

She laughed. "I know, but it was fun."

Raj snorted. "It was also sexy as hell."

"Hmm," Lyvia purred.

The two bears continued to fight in front of them. The female pinned the male down and bit his ear. The male screamed, and she let him go, then shifted back to human form.

"Let that be a reminder!" she roared at him. "No one cheats on me! **NO-ONE!**" she screamed, then stormed away toward the parking lot.

"Dustin needs to shift back!" Daryl hollered.

"Let me go," Shar said when she saw her mate pacing back and forth on the sidewalk.

Tate let her go, and she ran to her mate.

"Dustin," she whispered as she placed her hand on his shoulder.

Dustin growled when she touched him, then whimpered when she jumped back from him. The cougar moved toward his mate and rubbed his head against her chest.

Shar smiled. "You're so beautiful. But you need to shift before the cops get here," she said, rubbing the top of his head.

The cougar sat on his hind legs and started to shift.

"Dustin," Shar cried as she fell into her mate's arms.

"Sharissa," Dustin breathed, holding her close.

The sirens stopped, and two cars pulled up against the curb.

"Time for me," Tate said as he walked over to the four officers who stepped out of the cars.

"What is he going to do to them?" Shar asked as she watched.

"Make them forget what they saw. Make them believe it was just a regular bar fight, and it had broken up before they got here," Dustin said as he nuzzled her neck.

"How are we going to get **that** jackass to shift back?" Raj asked as he and Lyvia joined Dustin and Shar.

"Don't know and don't care," Dustin grumbled.

"I want to see your wrists!" a shifter who'd been fighting them growled as he walked up to the two couples.

Lyvia, Raj, Dustin, and Shar held out their wrists at the same time. Their palms up so the assholes could see their mate's names and leave them the hell alone.

The man's face paled, and he backed away. "I think it's time for me to go home." Hhe turned and took off at a run.

Lyvia and Shar giggled as they watched the shifter run down the street.

"I can't believe all this bullshit we go through. Maybe we should stay home from now on." Sharissa pouted.

"No way," Raj said with a wicked grin. "I'm not hiding, and neither is my mate." He pulled Lyvia closer.

"The other three took off when that one did." Dylan laughed as he joined them.

Tate walked over to them, and they watched as the police cars drove away.

"He still hasn't shifted?" Tate asked, his head nodding toward the bear sitting away from them, alone.

"Nope." Raj wrapped his arms around Lyvia and set his chin on the top of her head.

"I'll take care of it," Tate said.

They watched the vampire walk over to the bear. He looked the shifter in the eyes and said something they couldn't hear.

"How do we know we're not always under that man's spell?" Raj asked.

"Because we'd all be some form of walking zombies." Dustin laughed.

Raj snorted. "I guess."

The bear shifted into his human form, turned without a word, and left.

"What did you tell him?" Lyvia asked when the vampire rejoined them.

"To shift back and forget everything he'd seen and done tonight. To stay away from any Fated Mate he smells. Unless it's his own. And go home and not ever return to this bar," Tate said with a shrug.

"Will he listen?" Shar asked.

He better if he knows what's good for him," Dustin growled. He turned his head to his mate's neck and breathed in her scent.

"That's disturbing," Dylan said, making a face at his brother.

Dustin chuckled. "Just wait until you find your mate."

Think of what would have happened if Tate hadn't been here," Raj said, looking around at his friends.

"Dustin would have killed the bear. Shar would have gotten herself hurt trying to help him, and we'd all be in jail right now," Daryl said with a shake of his head.

"**Okay, tonight is going in my** 'never happening again' file," Shar said, a chill running down her spine.

"Babe," Dustin said, kissing her cheek. "You're mated to a shifter. Believe me, this will happen again."

"**Don't forget to change Symone's** bandage twice a day," Lyvia said as her mate tried to drag her out the door.

"She knows all of this, Lyvia. You've been repeating it for the past two days," Raj said as he finally got his mate to the door.

"So sweet," Lyvia said, looking up at her mate.

"Yes, I am. Now let's go."

"Symone, you listen to Sharissa and Dustin! I'll miss you all!"

"They know, come on," Raj said as he dragged her to the car.

Shar and Dustin waved to their friends as they pulled out of the drive.

"Are you sure you're okay with us watching Symone and her kittens until they return?"

Dustin smiled down at her. "She's feline, so of course I am. Now, if it had been a dog...."

Shar chuckled. "I don't see a tiger getting along with a dog."

Dustin chuckled. "Right, you are."

Game On

Do you think Symone will be okay?" Lyvia asked as she _turned_ in her seat and watched Dustin's driveway disappear.

Raj snorted. "You kidding me? You just left her with a cougar and his mate, who's expecting a cub. Those cats are going to be spoiled rotten."

Lyvia snickered. "You're right," she said, turning back in her seat.

"Are you going to be okay?" he asked, taking her hand in his.

She nodded. "Yep. I'm with you," she said with a bright smile.

"Good answer," he said, squeezing her hand.

"Are you sure you won't get in trouble for bringing me along?"

"That's what we have Tate for," he said with a smile.

"Oh yeah, the IOU, I promised."

He nodded. "Hopefully, he won't ask for anything outlandish."

She shivered. "He's a vampire. I have a feeling anything he does is outlandish."

Raj chuckled. "Yes, but he's loyal to his friends. So maybe he'll go easy on you."

"I never thought I'd be friends with a vampire or find my mate," Lyvia said, beaming at Raj.

He grinned back.

When they got to the airport, Raj parked his car in the lot with the rest of his team's vehicles. They dashed inside and barely got to their plane before they closed the doors.

"Next time, I'm packing you in a suitcase while you're asleep," Raj said when they got to their seats.

She chuckled as she sat down by the window.

"About time you got here," Alec said as he walked down the aisle toward them.

"Alec," Raj said with a smile. "I'd like you to meet my mate, Lyvia. Lyvia, this is the only other shifter on the team, Alec."

"Nice to meet you." Lyvia smiled as she held her hand out to the shifter.

"Damn, this is going to be trouble," Alec said, shaking her hand.

"What?" Raj asked.

"Look around you," Alec whispered. "The plane has shifters everywhere, and you brought your mate onboard. And she's in heat."

Raj looked around them and grunted. "Shit."

"I'm not in heat," Lyvia hissed.

Alec leaned in toward her and sniffed the air around her. "Trust me, honey, you're in heat."

Lyvia frowned.

"You should have left her at home," Alec said as he stood up.

"Can't," Raj said once he was close enough to his friend. "We'd both go insane." He held his wrists up for Alec to see. "You've read the same books I have."

Alec whistled as he looked at the markings on Raj's wrists. "Okay, so everything is true?"

Raj nodded with a smile. "Oh, yeah."

"Well, I guess I'll take this empty seat behind you. Just in case."

Raj nodded. "Thanks, buddy."

"Are we in danger?" Lyvia asked when Raj sat down beside her.

Raj smiled. "Just stay close to me."

Lyvia nodded as she leaned against him and closed her eyes.

"Knock her up, then you won't have to worry," Alec whispered into Raj's ear once they were in the air.

Raj nodded. There isn't anything he wouldn't want more than to do exactly that. But he must respect his mate's wishes. Not that **he** has much to say about it, anyway. He can't even wear a condom. And he knows she'd started the pill a few days ago. He'd found it in her top drawer. So, it's all out of his hands for now.

~🐾~

"Go, Raj!" Lyvia shouted as she jumped up from her chair to cheer for her mate.

The game was going excitingly well. They were ahead three to one, and it was the last quarter. Raj and his friend Alec made a goal. Lyvia jumped up and down, whistling and cheering.

Luckily, they hadn't had any trouble from the other shifters on the plane ride here. Also, luckily, that will be the only plane ride until they head home. Because even in sleep, she'd been nervous as hell that someone was going to kill Raj and his friend to get to her.

She knows Raj had seen the birth control pills in her top drawer; the clothes around them had been disheveled. She hasn't taken one yet; she's not sure if she doesn't want to start a family with her mate. Sure, they don't know each other that well yet, but he's her mate. What other man is she going to have a family with?

She watched the countdown for the end of the game for a minute, then her eyes zeroed in on her mate. He turned to her, blew her a kiss, then made the winning goal just as the buzzer went off.

They won five to one.

The crowd erupted with chants, and Lyvia grinned as she listened to the crowd chant her mate's name over and over.

"Did you see him blow that kiss at me?" a woman said from behind Lyvia.

"No, he was blowing a kiss at me," another said.

Lyvia turned to the voices and found six puck bunnies fighting over who Raj had blown the kiss to.

Lyvia grinned. "Actually, ladies, he was blowing it at me."

"Dream on," a bunny said with a snort.

"Hey, aren't you the slut who kept pressing her body against the glass last week? Yeah, like that will win Raj over," the bunny snorted.

Lyvia chuckled, then growled at them. All six women moved back away from her. She smiled, then headed toward the exit of the ice rink to meet up with her mate.

She could hear the bunnies close behind her and rolled her eyes.

"Raj, Raj!" the bunnies shouted as they pushed past Lyvia.

"That kiss was for me, wasn't it?" one of the sluttier bunnies purred as she took hold of Raj's arm and leaned against him.

But Raj only had eyes for Lyvia. "Actually, no." He pulled his arm free from the bunny's grasp. "It was for my girlfriend," he said as he moved toward Lyvia. "So, how was I?"

Lyvia grinned and kissed him. "Wonderful," she whispered against his lips.

"How did that slut's horrendous display last week win her a hockey player that no other bunny has bagged?" one of the bunnies whispered, not realizing that the two shifters could hear her.

Lyvia growled and went after them. Raj took hold of her arm and turned to the bunnies.

"I would appreciate it if you didn't call my girlfriend a slut or a bunny. She's neither. There is a connection to shifters and their Fated Mates that no human but a mate, him or herself, will ever understand." Raj sniffed the air and shook his head.

"Which none of you are. So back the fuck off and stop talking shit about my mate, or I'll have you removed from every game, and believe me, I have my ways," Raj finished with a growl.

All six bunnies paled as they looked at them. The glimmering silver of their eyes had all six bunnies freaking out.

"Oh my God, they're shifters," a bunny screeched.

The six females left in search of another player.

Lyvia chuckled. "Nice handling there, Romeo."

He laughed. "Come on, we've got to meet everyone on the bus in fifteen."

"Where do I wait while you're changing?"

"There's a lounge in the locker room. You can wait there."

She nodded. "Okay."

"I have to go to the after-party," he said as he showed her to the room. "But after that, I'm all yours." He gave her a devilish grin.

She smiled back. "The hotel is going to get complaints tonight because your playing has me all hot and bothered," she said, leaning against him.

Raj growled and kissed her quickly on the lips, then walked to his locker to change.

Lyvia chuckled. *He's in for a world of wonder tonight, and she's not stopping at one time. Maybe she **will** start a family with her mate. And they'll start on it tonight.*

~🐾~

The after-party went by too slow for Lyvia. She couldn't wait to get her hands on Raj and tear his clothes from his sexy as sin body. Once the party died down, she practically dragged him by his ear to their room.

"You're aggressive tonight," Raj said with a laugh as they entered their room.

"I want to start a family," she blurted out as she sniffed up his neck. "Tonight."

He paused. "Are you sure?" he asked, his hands slowly moving to hold her arms so she would stay still.

But she wouldn't have any of it. She took hold of Raj and turned him so fast that he lost his balance. She tossed him onto the bed and pounced on him.

"I told you the hotel would get complaints tonight," she said, sniffing him from his navel to his ear.

He grunted. "What about the pills?"

She paused and looked at him. "I knew you'd found them."

He grunted in answer.

"But yet you said nothing," she said as she licked his jaw.

Raj's tiger growled. "I told you it was up to you," he said as he grabbed hold of her hips to stop her rocking against his hard cock so he could talk to her.

He looked into her eyes. "Are you sure about this?"

She nodded, and Raj's heart soared. He'd been so sad when he'd found the pills. He feared she'd never be ready to start a family with him.

"I haven't taken one," she whispered into his ear, and his body quivered.

"You haven't?" he asked.

She shook her head, her hair flying around her face.

He smiled as he reached up and tucked the tendrils behind her ears so he could see her eyes.

"Why not?" he whispered.

She shrugged. "Because I wasn't sure if my feelings were real or just nerves. I mean, I didn't think I'd find anyone to spend my life with, let alone my mate."

He nodded. He felt the same way. "So, we're going to try for our own cub tonight, huh?" he asked with a cheeky grin.

She giggled. "Yeah, that was the plan. Now shut up and fuck me." She jumped and tackled him.

They growled, mewed, purred, and rolled around as clothes flew around the room.

Lyvia wasn't sure if her panties were pulled off or ripped off. Either way, they were naked, and then he was inside her, and thoughts of anything but her mate and this moment—left her mind.

He did as she told him and fucked her good and hard. He was so deep inside her that if they didn't create a cub tonight, something was wrong with her.

"Damn, Lyvia, you feel incredible."

She mewed as her back arched into his movements. He slammed deep and hard inside her, and she cried out his name when her orgasm took over her body and mind.

When she came down from the orgasm, he was holding her close and moving inside her as if he'd die if he didn't fuck her until they both collapsed from exhaustion.

"Lyvia!" he cried out as his body shook with his orgasm. "Fuck, yes!"

"Holy Fuck!" she cried out when another orgasm erupted from her body.

Raj chuckled at Lyvia's words as he returned to Earth, his cock still pumping his seed deep inside her. He pushed his hips forward several times before his knot stopped his movements.

"That was intense," she said, out of breath.

He grunted. "Yeah."

She wrapped her arms and legs around him. "Do you think we made enough noise?"

He laughed as he kissed her nose. "I think so."

She nodded. "Good, we'll do it again in thirty minutes."

He smiled down at her. "If we keep this up, they'll kick us out of here naked."

She grinned up at him. "Then we'll fuck on their front lawn."

He laughed so hard his side ached. What had he done to deserve this woman? God, he loves her. He paused. Damn, he really does love her. Go figure—he's head over heels in love with his mate.

~☙~

The next morning, they didn't have any complaints about them at the front desk, but they got many stares, and some of the women in the lobby licked their lips at Raj.

Lyvia grinned as she clung to his side and glared at the women. "Sorry, ladies, he's taken," she said with a smirk.

The women mumbled about him being a free spirit, and she turned on them with a growl.

"He may be a free spirit, as you say, but he's **my** free spirit. So, you bitches, back the fuck off!"

The women's eyes grew wide when Lyvia growled territorially.

"Lyvia." Raj chuckled as he took hold of her arm. He looked at the other women and saw the silver eyes and knew why she was being so territorial, and grinned.

Her tiger was standing up for her mate to the other shifters. Which just made him love her even more. Because wasn't that what he and Dustin were doing just a few days ago?

He looked at the other female shifters and smiled. "Sorry, ladies, but I've been claimed," he said, holding his and Lyvia's arms up.

The shifter females sucked in shocked breaths when they saw the bonded markings. Some of the women's heads angled down, and others looked off to the side. Two continued to stare at the markings.

"May I see?" one of the females asked.

Raj looked at his mate, then at the woman. "We have a bus to catch, but sure, you can have a quick look."

Lyvia snarled, but the woman didn't go for Raj; she took hold of Lyvia's hands and turned them palms up. She looked at the word UNITY on Lyvia's right wrist, then looked at her left wrist and read her mate's name, RAJ.

"You know why the name is on the left wrist, don't you?" the woman asked, smiling into Lyvia's eyes.

Lyvia shook her head, surprised at how nice the woman was. She noticed her silver eyes didn't look right to be a shifter.

"Because like the human's wedding band is on their left ring finger, this is directly connected to your heart." The woman smiled.

Lyvia smiled. "That makes sense."

"If love is not shared, you will go insane," she warned them.

"Don't have to worry about that," Raj said, pulling Lyvia to his side.

The woman smiled. "Yes, I see that. It's in your eyes," she said, then looked at Lyvia. "But you, my dear, you are still confused. You want to start that family with your mate, but what you're reading as something to make your mate happy, you're denying yourself that love."

Lyvia blushed, and Raj stared at her. Did she not love him?

"Don't take my word negatively, Raj Cunningham. She knows her own feelings. She just needs to understand them better. But you two better catch that bus," she said with a smile.

"You're not a shifter," Lyvia whispered.

The woman looked around them and then smiled at Lyvia. "Very perceptive."

"Witch," Raj said, taking a step back and pulling Lyvia with him.

The woman smiled and moved closer to them. "A white witch. You have nothing to fear from me. I just like to hide among the shifters. See what I can see."

"What do you see with us?" Lyvia asked as she pulled away from Raj and moved closer to the witch.

The witch smiled. "You're trying for that family, but it won't happen when you want it to. It will come to you when you are ready and no sooner. You are no longer in heat, so shifters should back down now."

"Thank you," Lyvia said, one eyebrow raised. "I think."

The woman chuckled. "Be safe, Lyvia. And remember that you don't have to fear your feelings."

Lyvia nodded and held her hand out to the woman. "Will I ever see you again?"

The witch smiled and shook Lyvia's hand. "I suspect you will. I see myself looking for something—which will bring me to you again. But you must go now; your coach is waiting for you."

"Damn it!" Raj growled as he took hold of Lyvia's arm and dragged her from the hotel.

"Wait, what's your name?" Lyvia called out.

'Pearl. My name is Pearl Owens. I will see you again, Lyvia Yule.'

Lyvia blinked. She has heard of witches invading minds like a vampire, except vampires can only penetrate a human's mind. Like Tate does with Shar. Except with Shar having Dustin's abilities and strength of body and mind, he can only vaguely read her mind.

He can't put thoughts into her head or completely take control of her.

Shifter in Heat

Did she do something to you? Raj asked, watching her face. If that witch harmed his mate, he's going to…

"No, no." Lyvia giggled. "She just sent me her name through my mind."

He sighed with relief. As nice as the woman was, he didn't trust witches. Even if she **is** a white witch.

"Where the fuck have you been, Cunningham!?" the coach shouted when Raj and Lyvia got to the bus.

"Sorry, Coach. Had trouble checking out," Raj said as he and his mate stepped onto the bus.

"I'm sure it had something to do with all the noise you two were making last night!" one of Raj's teammates shouted from the back of the bus, making everyone hoot and holler.

Raj saw Lyvia's cheeks turn a bright red and growled. "Can it—or I'll come back there and make you suck your own dick."

"Oooooooo," everyone said as they looked at the speaker in the back.

"It's okay, Raj." Lyvia took his hand and smiled at the others. "They're just jealous because you don't have to pay for sex. And you can have it whenever and wherever you want," she purred.

She smirked at him, then plopped herself down in an empty seat and pulled him down beside her. She leaned toward him, pulled him to her, and kissed him.

Shouts and whistles erupted, and the coach shouted for silence. "Please refrain from fucking your girlfriend on the bus, Cunningham!"

Raj chuckled as he pulled back from Lyvia's kiss and kissed her on the nose. "God, I love you."

She took a deep breath and laid her head on his shoulder. Raj sighed and kissed the top of her head; the witch said to have patience with her.

"I love you too," she whispered as she closed her eyes.

Raj grinned. *'Yes!'* he thought, then closed his eyes and laid his cheek against his mate's head.

The next few weeks went by fast. Raj was kicking ass on the ice, and they were fucking like rabbits in the hotels. But still, Lyvia wasn't pregnant. She feared she would never give her mate a cub, which put her into a depression.

She knows Raj could feel her depression, and when they made love, he made sure she was pleasured to the point of almost passing out. But it didn't stop her thoughts of how she's not a good enough mate. She can't even give him a cub.

"Lyvia," Raj whispered to her—three weeks after they'd started trying for a family.

"What," she sniffled.

He pulled her closer. "Remember what Pearl said? It will happen when we're ready."

"But I **am** ready, Raj. More than ready to have your cub." She sniffled.

He sighed heavily. "I know, Mafilia, I know."

"Maybe I'm defaulted, and you should trade me in for a newer model. I **am** eighty-eight years old, after all."

He shook his head. "So what? My mom was over a hundred when she had me. And I'm ninety-eight."

She chuckled. "We're a couple of old farts trying to start a family."

He snorted. "Watch who you call an old fart."

She giggled when he started tickling her.

"Besides," he said, gently kissing her. "Dustin is ninety-six."

She sighed. "With a twenty-four-year-old human as a mate."

Raj growled as he rolled her onto her back and pinned her to the bed.

"Enough of this pity party, Lyvia Yule. A **WITCH** told you that you will have my cub. We just have to wait for the right time."

She frowned. "It's been three weeks."

"Lyvia, you know I love you, but you're being nuts. We have two more games to win, then the championship. I don't want to worry about my mate while I'm playing."

Lyvia nodded. She has been selfish. Not only was he dealing with their lack of a family, but he also had hockey to think about. From now on, her mind will be on the game. **Then** she'll mope around about not giving her mate a cub.

"Okay, Mafilio. No more moping and whining. We concentrate on your games and continue to fuck like rabbits. Who knows, maybe it'll happen."

He grinned. "There's my mate. Come here."

She grinned with pleasure and, for the next hour, thought of nothing but her mate and what he does to her body.

"Go, Raj!" Lyvia called out two weeks later at the championship game.

She's so proud of him. And his team as well, of course. They're amazing on the ice. She can't wait until they have little ones cheering for their daddy as he skates around the rink like a pro ice skater shooting the puck into the net again and again. Oh God, and don't forget the slamming of players against the glass. Damn, that turns her on.

An odd feeling flowed through her body, and she doubled over.

'What the hell?'

A familiar scent filled the arena, and Raj looked up at the stands to his mate's seating area. She was bent over, her face making pain-filled looks.

"Damn it!" he cursed.

"Head in the game, Cunningham!"

Raj could barely breathe, and his tiger wanted out. He wanted his mate. Now!

"She's in heat again," Alec said as he skated over to Raj.

Raj nodded. "The first time was when we'd connected, so she hadn't felt the pain of it, just the hunger of wanting me," Raj said as he looked up at his mate again, who was in a lot of pain. "Only our mating can stop her pain," he growled.

Alec nodded. "But you can't screw her here."

Raj sneered. "I can't let the team down, either."

"Alec, Raj, get your asses off the ice—now!" their coach bellowed.

Raj and Alec skated over to their coach.

"I need a phone," Raj said as he climbed over the low wall.

"You don't need a phone!" the coach yelled. "What you need is to get your head on the championship!"

"Coach, with all due respect. If I don't use a phone, and soon. I will walk off this ice. Championship or no championship," Raj growled.

"Raj," Alec said, tapping his friend's arm.

"I mean it, Alec. Lyvia is more important…."

"I know, look." Alec pointed to where Lyvia stood in the stands.

"Mother Fuckers!" Raj roared when he saw several males approaching his mate. In her state of mind, she'll have a hard time fighting them off. "Give me your phone!" Raj yelled as he held his hand out to his coach.

The man was staring up at the stands where Lyvia was. "You can't go psycho on me because your girlfriend is a slut," the coach said.

Raj balled his fist to hit the man. Alec pulled him back.

"Hitting the coach won't solve your problem," Alec hissed in his ear.

"No, but it will make me feel soo good," Raj growled.

"You need to get your head in the damn game!" the coach said, looking from Raj to Lyvia and back again.

Raj turned to his mate and growled a feral growl that was heard in the stands. The men surrounding her paused when they heard it.

"Coach," Alec said with an unnatural calm. He knew his friend wouldn't be able to talk nicely to their coach at the moment. Not with his mate in danger in the stands. Raj moved to climb over the glass wall, and Alec stopped him. "We are not human, as you well know," Alec said as he pulled his friend away from the glass.

A cheer erupted on the other side, and the coach cursed. "They're winning because you two can't get your heads out of pussy…."

"My mate is in heat, and every asshole shifter in this place is going to try and rape her!" Raj yelled in his coach's face.

The man's face paled as he reached into his pocket for his phone. "Well then, why didn't you say so? You know I read up on shifters when you two joined the team."

Raj took the phone from his coach and dialed the one person he knew could help.

"Who the fuck is this, and how did you get my number?!"

Raj grinned. "I need your help. Now!" he hollered the last word into the phone.

The vampire appeared before him, and everyone in the area gasped.

"This better be important," Tate grumbled as he hung up his phone.

"Sniff the air and look up there," Raj said, pointing to his mate, where the shifter males were trying to touch her. She was fighting them off but just barely. Some left when she showed them her wrists, and others were too dumb.

Tate took in a deep breath and turned toward the stands. "You'll owe me again," he said, then disappeared.

Raj sighed with relief when Tate appeared beside Lyvia.

Lyvia jumped when she felt a hand on her shoulder. She turned and gasped when she saw the vampire.

"Tate," she cried out as she jumped into his protective arms.

"It's okay, little tiger," Tate said with a smile as he held her. He looked up at the four men licking their lips as if she was a three-course meal. He hates leches.

"You don't want any of this, boys," Tate said, looking into each of their eyes. "This young lady is protected by me and her mate. Unless you want to die, I'd advise you to leave."

"And what are you going to do about it, Vampire?"

"I will suck you all dry if you don't back the fuck off." Tate leaned in to look deeper into each of their silver eyes. "You really don't want that, now do you?"

"No, we don't want that," the four men said at the same time, then turned and left to return to their seats.

"Don't think that will be the last of them."

"What's happening?" Lyvia asked, her stomach tightening again.

"You're in heat, Lyvia, my dear," Tate said, holding her close.

"But… but it didn't feel this bad the first time," she said with a moan.

"Because you'd just found your mate and was in a fuck frenzy of sorts." Tate chuckled.

"Why does it have to hurt so much?" she asked with a gasp.

"Because it's your body preparing for the life you are supposed to create. I'd think you'd be having the Ice Star's cub by now."

Lyvia cried. "We've been trying."

Tate sighed. "It's the Goddesses. They have their hands on this one."

She looked up at him with an odd look, and he laughed as he kissed her forehead.

"Some other time, little tiger, some other time. Right now, how about we get you connected to your mate so the pain subsides?"

Her face brightened. "You can do that?"

He chuckled as he led her down to the glass. Raj appeared and pounded on the glass with his glove.

"Lyvia!" Raj hollered.

"Raj!" she cried out as she ran to the glass and pressed her body against it.

"I'm going to win this game for you, then we're going straight to the hotel." Raj watched Lyvia hump and practically rape the other side of the glass.

"Please," she begged, then licked the glass.

"Soon, baby, soon," he promised, then returned to the game.

Having Tate with his mate, he could concentrate on the game. Tate had been the first supernatural creature he could think of to help him. He was able to get to them fast, and his mate's pheromones won't affect him.

"Raj!" Alec yelled as he passed the puck.

Raj brought his thoughts fully to the game and was more determined than ever to win the game.

"He looks so sexy when he's on the ice," Lyvia said, then licked the glass again.

Tate chuckled. A hormone-ruled shifter is funny to watch. Too bad there's not more of them. Sure, shifters without mates go into heat. But nothing like a Fated Mate. Plus, he feels there's more to this little tiger than they know.

"Raj!" Lyvia screamed as she pounded on the glass. "Kick their asses so we can fuck!"

Tate laughed when he saw the look on Raj's face as his cheeks turned a bright red.

"Excuse me, ma'am. You can't be here...."

"It's all right," Tate said as he walked over to the human security guard and looked into his eyes. "Go back to your post; this young lady has permission to be here."

The man nodded. "Permission to be here," he said, then turned and walked away.

"Me and Shar should use you on our boss," Lyvia said, watching Tate.

"Oh?" Tate asked, intrigued.

Lyvia nodded. "Someone has been screwing with our reports, and the boss thinks all we need to do is fix it, but when we do, they mess it up again. He won't even look into it."

"Hmm." Tate smiled. "Sounds like a mystery to me. I'll think about it."

Her eyes widened. "Really?"

"Sure." Tate grinned. "I do love collecting IOUs."

She snorted. "Should have known it wasn't out of friendship."

Tate's heart ached at that. Okay, he hadn't realized the girls thought of him as a friend. How intriguing. "Maybe I'll do it as a favor to you and Shar. A present for the mommy-to-be."

She smiled at him, and his heart swelled. Okay, these shifters and human mates are getting to him. But surprising enough, he's not annoyed by it.

Lyvia screamed, which brought him back to what was going on. He looked around and found no attackers. Lyvia was pounding on the glass, cheering for her mate. He looked up at the scoreboard and saw that within the last thirty seconds of the game, Raj had slid the puck into the net—making the winning shot.

"Raj!" Lyvia screamed at the top of her lungs, making Tate cover his ears.

Raj threw his gear off in the middle of the ice once his teammates had set him down and skated over to the glass, where Lyvia was pressing herself against it again.

"Thanks, Tate," Raj said, smiling at the vampire.

Tate shrugged. "Just remember you owe me big time."

Raj nodded, then turned his eyes to his mate. "You ready, babe?"

Lyvia licked the glass, and Tate chuckled. "That's horny tiger speak for… *'Yes, baby, take me now.'"*

The White Witch's Dreams

"Careful, Mafilia." Raj laughed as they entered their hotel room, and Lyvia jumped on his back.

"Fuck me," she growled.

He chuckled. "I will as soon as I get out of my jersey. I didn't even have time to shower…."

"No shower!" she screeched, licking his earlobe.

Raj grumbled as he headed for the bed. He'd asked his teammates to gather his crap for him while he took his wild, sex-driven mate back to the hotel. Yes, of course, he's sex driven as well, but not as much as he'd been when they'd first found each other.

"Fuck me, Raj," she whimpered.

"I'm going to, baby, believe me, I am, but I stink…."

"You didn't care about stinking the first…."

He cut her off by tossing her onto the bed. "Actually, I did. Why do you think I was naked when you found me? I'd rushed into the shower before our friends got you to the locker room."

"Oh," she purred. "But I like it when you're all sweaty after winning a game."

He eyed her. "You do?"

She nodded as she got to her knees and started yanking on his jersey. "Very sexy," she said as she licked his sweaty stomach.

"Fuck, Lyvia."

"Yes, please fuck Lyvia," she purred.

He chuckled. "You're crazy when you're at the beginning of your heat. You know that?"

She nodded. "Fuck me."

He growled. "If you keep saying that, I won't be able to do any foreplay to get you wet…."

"Fuck me!" she screamed at the top of her lungs.

"Screw this," Raj growled.

He tossed his jersey to the floor and stripped out of his clothes. When he stood before her naked, she grabbed his throbbing cock and pulled him toward her.

"Now your turn," he said as he went for her clothes.

She shook her head as she grabbed his hips and pulled him down on top of her. He groaned when his cock almost slid instantly inside her.

"Lyvia…." All thought left his mind when she shoved down and impaled herself with his cock.

"Holy fuck!" she cried out.

He chuckled. He loved everything about Lyvia, even her strange quips.

"Lyvia," Raj growled, his tiger over-excited to be mating with their mate. He'd been the hardest to fight through this whole thing.

"Fuck me," she growled as she moved on his cock.

"Whatever my mate wants," he said as he grabbed her hips and moved fast and hard.

"Yes!" she cried out.

"Holy shit, you're tighter than usual tonight," he said as he picked up speed.

"I'm in heat," she whispered as if it was a secret.

He chuckled. He loved his mate when she was in heat. Almost as much as he loved her any other day.

"Raj!" she cried as she moved with him. "I'm going to cum!"

"Yes, please do," he grunted as he squeezed her hips and moved harder and deeper.

How he'd so easily ended up inside her with her clothes still on was beyond him. She must have dodged her panties on their way to the hotel.

She cried out his name, and her pussy tightened around him.

"Ah, fuck!" he growled.

Raj grunted and called out her name as he exploded inside her.

"Yes," she whispered with a purr, then was fast asleep.

"Lyvia?" he whispered, then chuckled.

He wrapped his arms around her and waited for his knot to loosen, then realized at that moment that if she never gave him a single cub, he would be happy to just spend his life with her. Fucking until they fell asleep; and loving each moment they were together.

~ 🐾 ~

"Lyvia!" Sharissa hollered as she wobbled to her friend when they walked in the door.

"Shar!" Lyvia said with excitement as she embraced her friend, then stood back and shook her head. "Look at you; you're so big."

Shar grinned. "Five and a half more weeks," she said, rubbing her large stomach.

"Do you know what it is yet?"

Shar shook her head. "We want to be surprised. So, we painted the nursery in blues and pinks to ensure we covered everything."

Lyvia chuckled. "Sounds lovely."

"It is," Shar said with pure excitement as she took hold of Lyvia's hand. "Come see."

Lyvia chuckled as her friend dragged her through the house and to the nursery.

Raj and Dustin walked into the house and found both their mates missing.

"Lyvia?" Raj called out.

Dustin chuckled. "Sharissa is probably showing her the nursery."

Raj smiled. "She must be huge by now."

Dustin grinned. "Oh yeah. And she's more beautiful than any woman on the planet."

Raj nodded. "I wish Lyvia, and I could have a cub. But it seems the Goddesses have chosen not to bless us."

Dustin shouldered his friend. "It may still happen."

Raj shrugged as he sat on the back of the couch. "Maybe. But if not, I am happy to live my life, just me and my mate."

Dustin nodded. "Spoken like a true Fated Mate. Have you guys said the L word yet?"

Raj grinned. "Yep, over a month ago."

"Good." Dustin nodded. "Because that's all you really need. Your mate's love. Cubs are just a bonus."

"Did you just call our cub a bonus?"

Raj and Dustin turned to their mates, and Dustin's cheeks turned bright red.

"A bonus next to you, Mafilia. We were discussing that we would be happy if we only had our mates in our lives. That cubs are just a bonus next to our beautiful mates."

"Nice save," Raj whispered.

Dustin grinned. "Always good to make a save with the truth."

Shar grinned and walked over to Dustin. "As long as you don't tell our cubs that."

Dustin nodded and pulled his mate into his arms. "It's between us," he said, then kissed her.

Lyvia looked at Raj, and Raj felt his heart skip a beat.

"Is that how you really feel?" she asked as she moved toward him. "You can live with it just being the two of us?"

Raj nodded. "Yes, Mafilia. You are my Fated Mate. You're all I need. I will love any cub you give me, but if I only have you, I will still be the happiest tiger in the world."

She grinned as she wrapped her arms around his neck. "You're all I need too."

Raj smiled and placed his hands on Lyvia's hips. "Are you sure you're not depressed anymore?"

She shrugged. "I'll always be sad that I can't give you the cubs you deserve. But I came to a realization while in my haze. I love you and need you, and I will be happy if it's only you and me, always and forever."

He grinned. "Sounds good to me," he said, then kissed her.

The doorbell rang, and everyone turned to the door.

"Who could that be?" Shar asked.

Dustin moved over to the door and opened it.

"Oh, hello, you must be Dustin," a familiar voice said from the other side of the door.

Lyvia moved out of Raj's arms and walked to the door to find a grinning Pearl on the other side.

"Pearl," Lyvia said, shocked to see the witch.

"Lyvia, so good to see you again," Pearl said with a bright smile.

"Dustin, this is a, uh…."

"Friend," Pearl said. "I'm Pearl Owens, and you must be Dustin Kraftman, mate to…." She looked around Dustin and spotted the very pregnant Sharissa. "Mated to the lovely human, Sharissa Flemmings."

"What the fuck?" Dustin stared at the woman, then looked at Lyvia and Raj. "What did you do? Tell her everything about everyone you know?"

"Oh no," Pearl said before the other two could answer. "We only talked for a few minutes, not enough time to learn anything. I have known about you two for many years. Actually, all four of you, but that's beside the point. I came to talk with Lyvia and Raj."

"You… What?" Dustin asked, confused.

Pearl smiled as she pushed past the confused shifter.

"Pearl is a…." Lyvia started to say but couldn't finish.

"A witch," Pearl said as if it was an everyday thing to find a witch in your house.

"A what!?" Dustin bellowed as he moved to stand between the witch and his mate.

Pearl waved her hand at him. "Don't worry, shifter. I won't harm your mate or your cub. I'm a white witch. Besides, I came to talk with Lyvia and Raj about their cubs."

"What cubs?" Lyvia asked with a squeal.

"Oh right, too soon." Pearl smacked herself in the forehead with her palm.

"What's going on, Witch?" Raj demanded as he stood up from the back of the couch.

70

Pearl smiled at them. "Please have a seat," she said as she motioned to the couch, then turned and looked at Shar and Dustin. "You too. You have a big role to play in this as well. Now come sit."

Shar looked at Dustin, who was still glaring at Pearl.

"She said white witch," she whispered to her mate.

She has read many books since she found her mate. And one of them was on witches and which ones to trust. And how to tell which ones are good. She pulled on Dustin's arm and whispered into his ear. He looked at her wide-eyed, then disappeared into the kitchen and returned with a bottle of bleach.

"What the fuck are you doing?" Lyvia screeched when she saw Shar with the bleach.

Pearl looked up at Shar as calmly as possible and watched the human pour the bleach over her arm.

"I knew you were the smart one." Pearl smiled.

"She's a white witch, all right," Shar said, then started coughing.

"Damn it, Shar, that was stupid. Bleach fumes can hurt you and the cub," Lyvia said as she moved over to her friend.

Dustin snatched the bleach bottle from his mate, capped it, and then tossed it out the door.

"Don't fret." Pearl snapped her fingers, and the air cleared, including the air in Shar's lungs. And the liquid on Pearl's arm evaporated. "No harm done."

Dustin pulled Shar into his arms. "Why didn't you tell me the bleach could harm you and our cub?"

Shar shook in her mate's arms, still scared that she hurt their cub with her stupidity.

"I-I didn't know," she cried against him.

"Shar, come here," Pearl said, curling her finger for her to move over to her.

Dustin stayed close to his mate as they walked over to the witch.

Pearl laid her hand over Shar's stomach and smiled. "Do you want to know the sex?"

"No," Shar and Dustin said at the same time.

"We want to be surprised." Shar smiled.

Pearl nodded. "Your cub is just fine. The fumes didn't make it past your lungs. Your lungs are clean and clear. Would you like to hear the heartbeat?"

"Yes," the mates said simultaneously, then laughed.

Pearl mumbled something, then a heartbeat echoed in the room. "Very strong heartbeat." Pearl smiled.

"That... that's our cub?" Shar asked, amazed at what they were hearing.

"Yes," Pearl said with a smile.

Dustin grinned as he pulled his mate's back against his chest.

"I will bring you something next time I come by, so you can hear your cub whenever you want." Pearl snapped her fingers, and the heartbeat stopped.

"Thank you," Shar said, tears in her eyes.

Pearl smiled. "You are most welcome."

"I want to know why Shar poured bleach on Pearl," Raj said, looking at where Shar had poured the bleach on Pearl's arm.

"Because if she was a dark witch, her skin would have bubbled and blistered, and she'd have killed me...." Shar's eyes opened wide. She'd almost gotten herself killed, ah shit.

"Killed you?" Dustin growled.

Pearl looked at them and smiled. "I think a dark witch would have backhanded you, Shar, but she wouldn't have killed you. You're a Fated Mate, which is against all laws of killing. If she killed you, she'd have to deal with the wrath of the Goddesses. Slapping you, she'd have dealt with the shifters and would have left before they could tear her head off."

Dustin grumbled as he pulled *his* mate closer.

"Sorry," Shar whispered, looking up at him.

The Omega

Dustin didn't respond to his mate's apology but held her closer and let her know with his eyes that she was not getting out of this so easily.

"But enough of that, let's get back to you two."Pearl turned to Lyvia and Raj.

"What did you mean by cubs?" Lyvia asked as she returned to her place on the couch.

"Well, I have been getting visions of the Fated Mates for hundreds of years now. When Dustin and Sharissa found each other, I got a dream about their cub. And knew they'd found one another."

"Are our children important?" Shar asked.

Pearl smiled at her. "Very important to the future of all of us."

"Who is all of us?" Dustin asked.

"The Supernaturals, of course," Pearl said with a smile.

"I'm not a Supernatural. I'm a human," Shar argued.

Pearl turned her head and smiled at her. "You are a Supernatural. You're a Fated Mate. Do you not have gifts beyond human abilities?"

Shar nodded. "I have my mate's abilities."

"All but shifting, yes." Pearl nodded.

"I'm a Supernatural?" Shar asked with wide eyes and excitement in her voice.

"Indeed." Pearl chuckled. "So back to why I'm here." She turned back to Lyvia and Raj. "Lyvia, I know you have been concerned about having your mate's cub."

Lyvia nodded. "Yes, we have tried and tried," she said with a frown.

Pearl smiled. "But as I told you, it wasn't your time."

"What does **that** mean?" Dustin asked.

Pearl looked back at Dustin, then at Lyvia and Raj again. "You two were thousands of miles from home. Raj was playing the games of his life. And you were there with him. Of course, you couldn't stay home, and traveling while carrying cubs is not safe."

"Cubs?" Lyvia asked, her voice squeaking.

"Yes," Pearl said, excitement in her voice. "I dreamed about them. And oh, girl, they're so beautiful." She turned to Shar and smiled at her. "So are yours."

"Do I have more than this one?" Shar asked, placing her hand over her stomach.

Pearl nodded. "Yes, you and your mate have more than one. But it's **this** pregnancy that's important." She smiled. "Your cub will lead them all."

"Ou-our cub?" Shar squeaked.

Pearl chuckled. "Yours **is** the oldest, after all."

"How many others?" Raj asked.

Pearl looked at him. "Several more Fated Mates, and each couple will produce the next step to the army...."

"Army!" Shar nearly screamed.

"Not the kind you think," Pearl said. "Your children are destined to save the world. Why do you think the Goddesses created Fated Mates? They know when they will be needed. That is why there haven't been any in so many years."

"Wasn't Tate's parents the last?" Dustin asked.

"Yes," Pearl said.

"But there was no war going on when Tate was born," Raj said. "There hasn't been in thousands of years. Not since...."

"Not since Christ, yes, I know." Pearl nodded. "Tate has a different fate in store for him."

"A different fate?" Dustin asked, confused.

Pearl nodded. "For one, helping you and your mates. If you will notice, he has a soft spot for Fated Mates. And his parents are a big reason for that. But also, it was born into him to protect the Fated Mates."

"He's a bodyguard, so to speak," Raj said with a nod.

"So to speak." Pearl nodded. "But he also has another position. I can't reveal it to you; it's too soon."

"Damn, this shit is confusing," Dustin said, collapsing into a chair. He turned and pulled Shar onto his lap.

"What is happening that the Goddesses created us for?" Lyvia asked.

"We won't know until the Goddesses feel fit to tell us," Pearl said. "When I know, I will be sure to tell all of you."

"What about our cubs?" Raj asked.

"Yes, your cubs." Pearl smiled. "The Goddesses knew you weren't ready. So, they blocked your conception while you were away. But now…." She pointed at Lyvia's stomach.

Lyvia wrapped her arms around her stomach. "No way," she said, her eyes large as saucers. "Holy fuck."

"But she just started her heat yesterday." Raj looked from his mate to the witch and back again.

Pearl chuckled. "And have you not noticed how much calmer she is now, after your first tryst last night?"

Raj grinned from ear to ear. "Just the once, that's all it took?"

Pearl chuckled. "That's all that was needed. Did it not only take once for Dustin and Shar once she stopped taking her birth control?"

Dustin and Shar nodded.

"We're actually going to have a cub?" Lyvia squealed with happiness.

Raj held her close and kissed her temple.

"No, Lyvia, you're not having **a** cub," Pearl said.

Lyvia's face fell. "But you said…."

Pearl took hold of Lyvia's hand and squeezed it. "Lyvia, you're the most special of the group."

Lyvia's eyes blinked. "How so?"

Pearl looked at Raj, then back at Lyvia. "Lyvia, how much do you know about your family's past?"

Lyvia shrugged. "Not much. They never really liked me because I was a girl. My dad only wanted boys."

Pearl nodded. "That's because the females on your dad's side of the family have a high chance of being what their ancestors were."

"I don't understand." Lyvia shook her head.

"Lyvia." Pearl scooted closer to Lyvia. "You're an Omega."

Lyvia's eyes grew wide, and her mouth fell open.

"Holy fuck," Raj said, jumping back from his mate.

Dustin stared at Lyvia from the chair as if she'd grown a second head, and Shar stared at everyone as if they'd all gone mad.

"I-I can't be," Lyvia cried. "No." She shook her head vigorously.

"What's an Omega, and why is Raj looking at Lyvia as if she's a foreign object?" Shar asked, watching her friends as they freaked out.

"An Omega is a rare female shifter that can carry more than one cub at a time like an animal. They're rare, and no one has seen one in hundreds of years," Dustin said, still staring at Lyvia.

Lyvia started crying.

"Raj," Pearl said, pointing to Lyvia.

Raj shook his head. What the fuck is wrong with him? What a dick he is for jumping away from his mate. So what if she can have a whole litter of cubs at once? She's his, and the cubs are theirs. He's going to love them all until the end of time.

He moved his legs to either side of his mate, then pulled her back against his chest and held her.

"I love you, Lyvia," he whispered into her ear.

"Even though I'm an Omega?" she asked, still crying.

He chuckled. "Especially because you're an Omega. Babe, that just means more kids...."

"Oh my God!" Lyvia cried out. "What will we do with so many cubs at once?"

"That's why you're starting The Fated Mates Club," Pearl said with a smile.

"You know about that?" Shar asked, sitting forward. Then she thought about it and sat back against her mate. "Of course you do."

"You have friends to help you." Pearl patted Lyvia's hand.

"How… how many?" Lyvia asked.

Pearl smiled. "Four. Do you want to know the sexes?"

Lyvia nodded and looked up at Raj. "Do we?"

Raj grinned. "Sure."

"Three boys and a girl," Pearl said, squeezing Lyvia's hand when she started to hyperventilate. "After they're born, you go on the pill if that's any help."

Lyvia laughed. "Sounds good to me. We'll wait until they're out of the house before we try again."

Raj chuckled as he kissed Lyvia's cheek.

"Well, I must be going now," Pearl said as she jumped to her feet.

"Stay for lunch?" Shar asked, getting to her feet.

"Wish I could." Pearl smiled at them. "But people are headed this way, and I can't meet them. It's not our destiny to meet yet." She pulled a pair of sunglasses from her purse and placed them on her face. "If you have any questions or ever need me, give me a call." Cards appeared in their hands. "Take care," she said, then rushed out the door.

Pearl quickly walked down the path toward the driveway as four shifters walked up. She avoided looking at them as she hurried past them. Pearl sensed one of them stop and look at her as she made her way to her car. If only she hadn't driven here, she could have poofed out of here before they arrived.

"Hey!" he hollered after her. "Don't I know you?!"

Pearl closed her eyes and unlocked her car without using her keys. She got into her car as fast as possible and sped out of the driveway without answering him. She watched him in her rearview mirror. He shrugged, then turned and walked up the path to the door.

She took a deep breath to calm her nerves. "It's not our time yet, my love," she whispered, then concentrated on the road as she headed to her next stop.

"So, what do you truly think about what I am?" Lyvia asked Raj later that night as they got ready for bed.

Symone and tiger were settled back into her home, and Angel was with Shar. While she was gone, the kittens had gone and grown up. She doesn't want to miss anything like that again. But she won't ask Raj to quit what he loves.

"I'm happy, Lyvia."

She turned to him. "You're happy that I'm having not one, not two, not three, but **four** cubs?"

He chuckled. "Lyvia. They're a part of you and a part of me. I would be happy if you were having **eight** cubs."

She grunted. "No, you wouldn't. But nice try."

He growled as he jumped on the bed and pulled her down with him.

She giggled as he kissed her.

"Lyvia. I love you. And I love our four little tigers," he said, rubbing her stomach. "You and I were destined to have these cubs. Did you not hear what Pearl said?"

She smiled as she pushed a lock of hair behind his ear. "I love you too. But four?"

He grinned. "Whatever the Goddesses need them for. They will be a fearsome team."

She laughed. "Team, huh? Are you looking for a hockey team?"

He shook his head. "I'm putting hockey on the back burner for now."

She gasped. "Don't do that…."

He kissed her to silence her. "It's already done. I called earlier…."

"Oh, Raj. Call them, tell them you've changed your mind…."

"Lyvia. You can't travel while pregnant, especially with four. And you know we can't be separated. It's only for a year or two, maybe three."

She started to cry, and he pulled her against him.

"It's **my** choice Lyvia. Once the cubs are old enough to travel with us, I'll think about hockey again. Besides, it's not like I'll be too old in ten or twenty years to start playing again. And maybe our boys or even our daughter will pick up the sport."

She chuckled. "Nice save there."

He chuckled. "I would be **proud** if our tigress took a liking to sports like her old man."

She smiled. "I love you so much."

He kissed her hard and deep. When he came up for air, they were both breathing heavily.

"I love you more than my own life, and I will give you and our cubs everything I have."

She smiled up at him as she gently ran her fingertips down his jaw.

"All we require is your love."

This book may be over but their story is not.

NEXT SERIES LOADING….GET IT

Bonus Chapter

-While Lyvia is off with Raj for his games-

Sharissa set the pan on the counter and smiled. She's been having the strangest cravings. She looked at the brownies that were filled with peanut butter and strawberry jam. Okay, so it's not the best combination, but fuck, she wanted a piece of it. She cut into it and lifted a piece—burning her fingertips.

"Damn it," she cried as she dropped the square of brownie. The gooey center oozed over the top of the other brownies, and her eyes brightened. "Perfect!" she screeched.

When Dustin walked into the kitchen, she was spreading the strawberry jam over the (once again perfect pan of brownies). He stopped and stared at the pan.

"What in the world did you bake this time?"

His voice had her jumping. She turned around and grinned at her mate, the butter knife she'd been using to spread the jam in her hand—which had automatically come up in self-defense. The jam slid down her fingers, but she didn't notice as she stared into her mate's eyes. She's so in love with this man, **her** shifter.

Dustin grinned when he saw the look of pure lust in his mate's eyes. He also saw love and his heart swelled. Dustin walked over to Shar and took her hand into his. She continued to stare into his eyes as he pulled her hand to him and sucked one of her jam-covered fingers into his mouth. He moaned, and she shivered.

When he let her finger go, her cheeks were almost as red as the jam still dripping from the knife.

Dustin smirked as he brushed his finger against her hot cheek. "Strawberry jam, my favorite."

She smiled as she leaned her cheek into his touch.

He looked at the pan again and shook his head. "What have you baked this time?"

Shar shook her head and cleared her thoughts. "Peanut butter and jelly brownies."

Dustin choked out a laugh. Her odd cravings have given them plenty of strange new things to try.

"You don't get any," she said, pointing the knife at him. "If you laugh at me."

He looked at her and shook his head. "I'm not laughing at you, Mafilia. I am laughing at your odd cravings."

She snorted. "Same thing." She went back to spreading the jam across the brownies.

Once she was through, she lifted one out and took a bite. She closed her eyes with a sigh.

"Good?" he asked, watching her.

She opened her eyes and nodded. "Best thing I've come up with," she said, offering him a bite.

Dustin grinned as he leaned forward and took a bite. He chewed it for a minute, the flavors fighting in his mouth for dominance. It actually wasn't too bad.

"So?" Sharissa asked, watching him chew the bite of brownie.

Dustin smiled. "Better than the fish lasagna, but not as good as the pumpkin meringue pie."

Shar grinned and took another bite of the brownie. He hadn't liked her lasagna. She'd had to eat it all herself—not that she complained.

"Mom is coming over today," Dustin said as he leaned his hip against the counter.

Shar looked at him, then at herself. "When?"

He looked at his watch. "In about an hour."

Shar's eyes opened in horrification. "I'm a mess!"

Dustin chuckled. "I don't think she'll care."

Shar grunted as she shoved the rest of the brownie into her mouth. "Put that away for me," she said through the chocolaty goodness in her mouth, pointing to the pan of brownies.

Dustin grinned as he watched his mate run from the kitchen. They have plenty of staff who could fix her anything she wanted. When they refused to make some of the dishes she craved, she started making them herself. He didn't blame his staff. Some of the things she has asked for would make anyone run for the hills. All except for his beautiful mate. He sighed as he lifted the pan of brownies and placed them in the fridge.

He knows she'll have them finished before tomorrow. She was getting a shifter's appetite with the pregnancy. He chuckled when he thought of the other day when they were thrown from yet another buffet. His little pregnant mate had cleaned them out of almost everything in less than an hour.

"Do you need anything, Mr. Kraftman?"

Dustin turned to the maid and smiled. "Can you please clean up after my mate?"

The woman smiled and nodded, happy to have something to do. Since Shar moved in, there was less and less for his staff to do—because Shar can be a neat freak.

He'd thought about letting his staff go, but they're all shifters who need work, and with Sharissa pregnant, they could use the help. They stay out of sight and out of mind. Which Dustin appreciated, but he knew they were there because the house stayed clean. Luckily, they've always given him his space, or he and Shar would have been caught more than once fucking in one room or another in his mansion.

The doorbell rang, and he rushed out of the kitchen to answer the door. When he opened the door, his mother stood on the other side, beaming at him. She threw herself into his arms, and he chuckled as he hugged her.

"You're early, Mother."

Amirah Kraftman smiled as she hugged her second eldest. "I couldn't wait to see you and your lovely mate."

Dustin chuckled. He knows why she's here. Because Shar is pregnant with her first grandcub.

"Where is she?" Amirah asked as she moved past her son and into his large mansion.

"Taking a shower. She was a bit of a mess after making another of her concoctions."

Amirah turned to her son with a chuckle. "Is she at the crazy cravings stage?"

Dustin chuckled and nodded. "She is."

"What did she concoct today?" Amirah asked as she walked over to a couch and sat down.

"Peanut butter and jelly brownies."

Amirah's left eyebrow raised. "Inside or on top?"

"Both," Dustin chuckled. "Peanut butter and strawberry jam inside and jam over the top."

Amirah nodded. "I hadn't put jam on top. I covered it with peanut butter."

Dustin stared at her, his mouth gaping open.

Amirah chuckled. "Your cub has the same cravings you did when I was pregnant with you."

Dustin's mouth closed, and a grin spread across his face.

"Amirah," Shar squealed when she entered the living room and found Amirah sitting on the couch talking with Dustin.

Amirah looked up at Shar and smiled. "You look absolutely gorgeous."

Shar blushed. She knows she doesn't. Her hair is wet and lying straight down her back, and her clothes are sticking to her damp skin.

Amirah walked over to Sharissa and pulled her into a hug. "Motherhood looks divine on you."

Shar smiled as she hugged the woman back.

Amirah stayed for a few hours. She told Shar stories of when she was pregnant with each of her sons, especially Dustin. She ate lunch with them and sat out back while they discussed the playground Dustin wanted to build in the backyard. When it was time for her to leave, Shar was sad to see her go.

"I'll come for another visit, I promise," Amirah said with a grin. "And I will see you this weekend for family night. You're not missing another one." She turned to Dustin and gave him the evil eye.

They hadn't been to a family dinner since they'd discovered Shar was pregnant.

"Promise," Shar confirmed.

Amirah nodded, then pointed to Shar's stomach. "Take care of my grandcub."

Shar nodded. "Count on it."

Amirah grinned. "I'll give you the recipes I came up with while pregnant with Dustin. It seems your cub has its father's appetite."

Shar chuckled. "I'd love that."

Amirah hugged them and then left.

Shar looked at Dustin. "What now?"

Dustin grinned. "Bedroom." he lifted her into his arms and carried her up the stairs.

Shar giggled as she held onto him.

~🐕~

Shar was in the kitchen going through the cookbook Amirah had given her at the family dinner last night when she heard a loud noise outback. She set the book down and walked toward the door.

A loud growl and a hiss had her pulling the door open. She found Symone hovering over her kittens as she hissed and swatted at a dog, trying to get to the little ones.

Shar walked down the stairs faster than she should have and stopped when the dog looked up at her with a feral growl.

"Evil mutt," Shar growled at the dog.

With the dog distracted by Shar, Symone jumped onto the dog's head, hissing, and clawing.

Shar noticed the blood dripping into the dog's eye and almost screamed when the dog shook his head, tossing Symone across the yard.

"Symone!" Shar cried out. She headed toward the cat, but the dog turned to her and growled, foam dripping from his mouth. "Ah fuck," she whispered.

The kittens meowed and scurried over to Shar. As if they knew she would protect them while their mother was down.

"Get out of my yard," Shar growled at the mut.

The foaming mutt moved toward her. It stopped when Shar crouched in a defensive position and snarled. The dog snarled back and shook his head, spit flying everywhere. He moved to jump at her and stopped with a small whimper.

Unknown to Shar and unseen by anyone, her eyes flashed silver for a split second.

The mutt growled and jumped at her again. Shar prepared for the pain but was shocked when a wolf came out of nowhere and took the mutt down. She watched the wolf take hold of the mutt's neck and shake his head. She heard the snap of the mutt's neck and placed her hand to her throat as she stood from her defensive crouch.

The wolf turned to her, and she could see the kindness in his silver eyes. He shifted to his human form, and Shar sighed with relief. It was Dustin's gardener.

"I'm sorry I didn't get here sooner, ma'am," he said with a slight bow.

Shar smiled. "You got here just in time, Fredrick."

Fredrick grinned. "You know my name."

Shar nodded, and before she could say anything else, Dustin burst from the house and stopped at the top of the stairs, taking in everything in his backyard.

"Fredrick?" he asked his gardener.

"It's my fault," Shar said, smiling up at her mate.

Dustin looked at Sharissa, his left eyebrow raised.

"I will take care of this," Fredrick said as he picked up the dead mutt and walked into the woods to bury him.

The kittens' mewing caught Shar's attention, and she remembered Symone. She ran to the cat, who was still lying on her side, not moving.

"Oh, Symone, please be okay. Lyvia will never forgive me," Shar cried.

Dustin followed his mate and the kittens to where the mother cat lay motionless.

"What happened?" he asked, standing behind her.

Shar moved the cat and sighed with relief. She was still alive. But was she okay?

"We should take Symone to the vet," Shar said as she lifted the cat into her arms.

Dustin frowned. "What happened, Sharissa?"

Shar looked at her mate and frowned, then told him everything.

Dustin sighed. "Remind me to give Fredrick a raise." He wrapped his arms around her and walked her to the house.

They situated the kittens in a room, then headed to the car to take Symone to the vet.

~🐾~

The vet gave Symone a clean bill of health. She had a few bruises, but nothing was broken. When they got home, they placed Symone in the room with her babies, then headed to their room.

"Now for your punishment," Dustin growled as he walked up behind his mate.

Shar spun on him, her eyes open wide. "You wouldn't dare."

He frowned. "Sharissa. You almost got yourself **and** our cub killed."

Shar frowned. "I was protecting Symone and her babies."

Dustin sighed. "Their lives aren't more important than you or our cub."

Shar's frown deepened. "They aren't any less important, either."

Dustin growled. "Sharissa."

"Dustin."

Dustin pinched the bridge of his nose. "What punishment should I give you for your recklessness?"

Shar shrugged. "I didn't know he had rabies until after I joined Symone and her kittens."

Dustin sighed. "Exactly. Recklessness."

Shar looked down at her stomach. He was right. She shouldn't have jumped in like that without knowing what she was getting into.

Dustin pulled her into his arms. "Your punishment will be torture."

She stared up at him, her eyes open wide. "T-t-torture?"

He grinned. "Don't worry, Mafilia, it will hurt me as much as it will hurt you."

She blinked. How the fuck will **her** torture hurt **him**?

~❦~

She found out that night. Every time she was about to orgasm, Dustin would back away from her pussy. Then he would go at it again, bringing her to a boiling point, then releasing her before she could cum. He did it for hours, and she was about to commit murder.

She could see in his eyes that it was hurting him as much as it was hurting her. And she smirked.

After three hours of torture, Dustin finally had enough of the torment and figured it was enough punishment. He let her orgasm, then slammed into her so hard she screamed. He grinned as he slammed into her again and again. The tension from not letting his mate orgasm was too much for him. He came so hard that if she wasn't already pregnant, he knew she would be now.

"What the fuck was that?" Sharissa cried out.

Dustin snorted. "I don't think this was a good punishment."

She chuckled. "Why? Because you were punished as well?"

He grunted. "Because I don't think it has taught you a lesson to behave."

She groaned. "Well, that was the best sex we've ever had. Maybe I'll be bad more often."

Dustin chuckled. "I love you."

Shar grinned. "I love you too, Mafilio. More than words could ever say."

He smirked. "Even after your punishment?"

She chuckled. "The after-effects were worth it."

He shook his head. "You are one crazy woman."

Her eyebrow raised. "Didn't you already know that?"

He nodded. "Sadly, I did. Because who else but a crazy woman would so easily give herself to a man like me?"

Shar placed her hand to his cheek. "Our union may have been fast and crazy as hell. But I wouldn't trade it for the world. I love you, Dustin, and **nothing** will ever change that. You're my other half, my soulmate."

Dustin smiled. "And you are mine. For now, and all eternity."

"How many cubs do you want?" Shar asked out of the blue.

Dustin looked at her, his eyebrow raised. "How many do **you** want?"

She scoffed. "I asked **you** first."

He grinned. "At least four."

She smiled. "I think we're a perfect match, Dustin Kraftman."

Dustin leaned down as best he could (he was still knotted inside her) and kissed the top of her stomach.

"You and our cub are my everything, Sharissa. I love you both so much."

Shar smiled. "And we love you," she said as she slid her fingers through his hair. "Even if the Goddesses hadn't thrown us together, I think we'd have found each other one way or another."

He chuckled. "You **did** come to us to help you get away from your crazy ex."

She nodded and closed her eyes. If that man hadn't mentioned the Kraftman brothers, she would have never thought of them… Was **that** the Goddesses' way of throwing them together?

Dustin's cock made a noise when it popped out of her, and she giggled.

Dustin chuckled as he moved to the head of the bed and laid down. He pulled her against him and sighed heavily.

"Thank you," Shar whispered.

Dustin pressed his cheek to her head. "For what?"

"For being you," she whispered, then fell asleep.

Dustin sighed. "No, Mafilia." He kissed her forehead. "Thank **YOU**."